THE

DEATH

OF

LIFE

Praise for *USA Today* bestseller Pamela Crane's psychological thrillers:

"Her writing is dark, intriguing and she is a master of the unexpected twist. Ms. Crane cleverly blends a series of plots and subplots together to produce a satisfactory ending. Not all questions are answered and I'm looking forward to the next book in the series." – Peter Ralph, white-collar crime fiction writer, author of *Blood Gold in the Congo,* #1 Amazon best-selling author

"Pamela Crane introduces a mind-twist that takes everything you love about thrillers, pushes it outside the box, and electrifies you with clever prose and a plot that will terrify you. A must-read thriller...an instant best seller!" – Southern Editor Reviews

"A captivating mystery with prose that fans will devour." – Literary Lover Reviews

"If *Dexter* and *Gone Girl* had a love child, this would be it!" – reader review

"An author to watch, Pamela Crane packs a punch to her prose and will keep you on your toes with her twisted plots. Let your mind be blown—I guarantee you'll savor every moment. Psychological thriller fiction at its best." – Thriller Fan Reviews

"I'm a die-hard thriller fan. But Crane duped me! Just when I thought I had figured it out I was thrown for another loop...and loved it. Kudos to mastering the mystery genre!" – reader review

THE DEATH OF LIFE

PAMELA CRANE

Rockin' C Reads
Raleigh, North Carolina

Thank you for supporting authors and literacy by purchasing this book. Want to add more gripping reads to your library? As the author of more than a dozen award-winning and best-selling books, you can find all of Pamela Crane's works on her website at www.pamelacrane.com.

This book is dedicated to all those fighting for justice in an unjust world. For the foster children, the victims, and the beautifully broken, my story is for you.

*The fear of death follows from the fear of life. A man
who lives fully is prepared to die at any time.*
— Mark Twain

Chapter 1

Durham, North Carolina
Three months ago ...

It was the end of my life. The beginning of death. You don't know pain until you've felt the pinch of a blade against your neck, the edge shivering against your skin, ready to slice you open like a ripe peach—and you're the one holding the knife.

I was a tremble away from killing myself.

Two years ago I first noticed the shift within me. The slither of self-loathing snaking its way through me. My desire to live slipping away. Life had become unbearably heavy. A burden I wanted to drop like a dead body. Me being that body, of course.

But I didn't give up on life back then. *You're stronger than this urge,* I told myself. *You have a reason to live,* I whispered in the deep of night, but no one was there to hear me. No one heard my cries from the shadows. I thought I'd be okay, normal. But in my churning gut I knew better. A reason to live had died with my soul. As for the one who had shredded my soul? He was the man kneeling before me, sobbing. Beside him on the floor sat a roll of duct tape and some old rope that I'd found in the garage. I'd planned to bind him, but I didn't end up needing to.

He was a willing victim. All he wanted was the guilt to end.

All I wanted now was blood. The blood of one person in particular—Scott Guffrey.

For two years I fought the urge to kill him. For two years I battled with my sanity, trying to understand why. Why he had done what he did—a crime against humanity, a theft of innocence. For two years only silence echoed back at me.

That was when I realized the only path to numbness was in death. Scott's death. My own death. It felt conclusive, the right thing to do in a world full of so many wrongs.

Now I had him. After drinks at the bar, it didn't take long for Scott to get falling-on-his-ass drunk. "You can't drive home like that," I'd told him when the bartender with the sequined top announced last call for alcohol.

"You gonna drive me?" I stepped back from his yeasty beer breath as his head wobbled uncomfortably close to mine.

"Sure. Let's go." Guiding him like a lamb to the slaughter had been too easy. I almost felt bad. Almost. After talking to him for a couple hours, his humanity peeked out. I'd seen this easygoing, entertaining side of him many times before—always quick with a joke, good for a laugh and a pair of arms on moving day. A reliable friend to everyone; who didn't like Scott Guffrey? But we both knew the truth. That's the problem with getting to know your prey—you almost begin to like them. I had to keep my head clear. He was no human. Scott was a monster, and monsters needed to be put down.

Here we were, an hour and several emptied shot glasses later, after Scott had passed out on his scratchy blue sofa watching *The Good, the Bad and the Ugly* on a 46-inch plasma television that had been state-of-the-art over a decade ago. I thought the hardest part of the whole thing would be binding him without waking him, but it turned out to be shockingly unnecessary. I had forgotten what a heavy drinker—and sleeper—he was. Plus, it didn't hurt that I had slipped a roofie in his Jägermeister.

Sure, it would have been easier to kill him while he slept. But that wouldn't have been fair. I wanted him to know why he deserved to die. I wanted him to feel the gavel of justice pound down on him, the heat of my fury as I took his life like he had taken mine. A cup of cold water flung in his face forced him awake, sputtering slurred obscenities.

Then I froze as he fell to his knees on the poorly laid faux hardwood floor, still woozy from the Jager shots I'd been pouring down his throat for the past hour. I leaned over him and aimed the tip of the blade at his heart, then … nothing.

I couldn't do it. My knife was stoic, but my limbs were flaccid.

Going through with killing him—it a demon I was afraid to unleash. A creature that maybe I couldn't harness. I thought I was prepared for this moment. I spent weeks mentally hardening myself. Now that the time had come, I couldn't follow through. I was weaker than I thought.

"Look what you've done to me," I blurted. His eyes remained fixed on the floor. "Look at me!"

His body jumped at my demand.

His eyes peered hazily up at me. "I'm sorry," he said, shaking his head. "I wish I could take it all back." Tears pooled in the sunken craters of his cheeks.

He'd aged two decades in the past two years, I suddenly realized. His curly blond hair, once so abundant, was thinning and shot with gray. His ruddy complexion had been the picture of health. Now his jutting brow and cheekbones threatened to poke through the sallow skin of his gaunt face. Most striking of all, his blue eyes, once as bright as sapphires, were dull points of light set in black pits. I wondered if, like me, he suffered from chronic sleeplessness. I begged for it to stop—the disconnected thoughts rattling through my brain like a runaway freight train hurtling hell for leather toward an abandoned trestle. Why, oh God, couldn't I have peace? I hadn't done anything wrong ... until now. Scott, on the other hand, had plenty of guilt to keep him company.

In the drunken tears I saw a glimmer of true remorse, an acceptance of responsibility for what he'd done. I wondered how genuine it was when the shame was swimming in alcohol, but did it matter? An apology couldn't fix my broken mind, stop my nightmares, or deliver me from the darkness that engulfed me. Maybe death was too good for him. Maybe I was the one who needed it more than him.

It sounded so good at that moment.

I pressed the knife to my own throat. All I could think about was the past two years of anguish and suffering, and I knew killing him wasn't the answer. Killing myself was. But why should I be the one to die? I didn't deserve the punishment for the crime. Scott did. He should repent to his Maker, not me. The whimpering fool kneeling before me, he was the one who should pay the price. And I would help him pay it. For the rest of eternity in hell.

Then after this I would join him.

I knelt down and gazed into the mirror of his hazy eyes at the reflection of my own broken soul. I turned the knife on him, the blade a whisper away from his cheek.

"Tell me why I shouldn't kill you right now," I demanded.

A grown-ass man weeping on the floor. He was pathetic.

"Please," he begged. "Do it. I'm ready." The slur of alcohol left his speech now. There was nothing like a near-death experience to sober you up.

"What?" I asked. I hadn't expected him to say that, to want to die.

"I'm tired of it all. Of thinking about what I did. Of all the regret. The guilt. Just … make the pain stop."

He was begging now, and nausea bubbled up in my stomach like shaken soda spurting from a can. I couldn't let him get another word in, partly because I was afraid I'd chicken out. Partly because I wanted to chicken out. He would be my inauguration as a killer, a milestone I didn't want to celebrate. But today I had to.

"As you wish."

I grabbed his hair to steady him and swiped the knife across his throat. He dropped face-first like a sack of potatoes at my feet. I scurried back to avoid stepping in the blood pooling around him.

I didn't know how to describe what I felt at that moment. There's no way to put in words the emotions roiling through you when you realize you've done something you can't take back. When you realize you've just played judge, jury, and executioner in a single action, a swift motion of the arm. It was both horrifying and empowering. For a brief moment I feared myself—what I was capable of. Then the moment passed.

Looking down at the body of the man I just killed, his blood seeping into the gaping seams between the flooring, a haze of emotions swept over me. It was overwhelming, empowering, frightening … all too much at once. The sickness rumbling in my gut intensified, and my heartbeat quickened with a sense of panic that someone would show up and find me here with a dead man at my feet.

Relief—that sole word captured how I felt as I slipped out the back door into the pre-dawn gloom. No morbid pleasure in his death. Every day for two years a part of me wanted to die. Every morning I struggled to draw that first breath. Every evening I tossed in my bed mourning the life I lost because of him.

It was over. I had killed the thief who stole my hope. My soul had been dead for two years. But now suddenly I felt alive. Life for death. Death for life.

Chapter 2
Ari Wilburn

Present day
Durham, North Carolina

If you've never lived life "in the system," you wouldn't understand the dread that follows you with each sunrise. That dread soon becomes a part of you, burrowed so deep that you can't find the place where you end and the dread begins. While normal children in their normal lives wake up knowing what a normal day will bring, the luxury of "normalcy" left the moment my parents put me in foster care.

At age ten, not only did I lose my sister, Carli, to a horrible accident planned by a sadistic child trafficker who wanted to send my father a message, but my parents simply couldn't stomach having me around. With the blame of Carli's death hefted on my small shoulders, Mom and Dad banished me from the only family I knew and loved. After that, love became a distant memory. I spent my adolescence yearning for death to free me from the chains of life, and my adulthood stumbling around for purpose that I didn't really think existed—until I started a suicide support group and met a sex-trafficked girl named Tina Alvarez.

I'm sure it's not the healthiest of friendships—both of us emotionally bankrupt and lugging baggage so heavy that it would scare most people off—but when you've been friendless your entire life like we were ... well, when someone comes along who gets you, who wants you close, who cares about you, you don't let them go. Call it desperation, call it impulsive, call it what you want, but Tina was my salvation and I was hers. Our shared hurts magnetized us in a connection that only two wounded birds like us understood.

Friends come slow and easy for most people as they pick and choose and ease in, testing the waters with their toe. For me and Tina, it was like we'd scrambled into the same leaky lifeboat, doomed to sink, only to realize that by happily clinging to each other, we could survive.

Together we found Tina's trafficker, George Battan, and put him behind bars, but in the process we unearthed more secrets than answers. My own parents had a connection to George, but the extent of their involvement was uncertain. And Tina knew George ordered the death of a little girl named Marla Rivers, another victim Tina was trying to help escape, but the evidence simply wasn't there.

Rich criminal masterminds had a way of keeping their hands clean of such atrocities. But I'd dig until I hit pay dirt that would put him behind bars for life.

Have you ever wanted something so badly you'd do anything for it? Disown your family? Sell your soul? Kill? I've wanted a lot of things that I'd do just about anything to get. Breaking out of the foster system. Avenging my sister. Reuniting with my parents. Uncovering the truth about my family's secrets. Finding purpose in life. Until recently I never knew how far I'd go to get what I wanted. As a disgruntled teenager I'd almost killed myself for freedom from my self-loathing. As an adult I hunted down a killer to find peace for my murdered sister. But finding my purpose ... that was an itchy question. How could I scratch the surface of finding purpose in a life that tried to drown me in its misery?

It's corny but true, that every dark cloud has a silver lining—that spot where the sun pushes its way through. Tina Alvarez was my silver lining. And Tristan Cox was my sun. Sometimes I think that I was destined to meet them, if you believe in that sort of thing. And after twenty-four years, I met my true self for the very first time.

My purpose was to investigate the truth, unravel the answers. Closure was all I ever wanted for my own life, and now that I saw hope return to Tina's once dull eyes, I knew it was a gift I could give to many other victims of suffering.

Purpose became my lifeboat. It was my rebirth, my second chance. For some unfortunate souls, they never live, only enduring an endless torrent of days mildly better than dying. I was one of the lucky ones, at last prying off the fangs of pain so that I could genuinely live.

The sun rose this morning with nothing better to do, and I rose with it, feeling the warmth of a new day where my apartment wasn't so crappy, my car wasn't such a piece of junk, my life wasn't so bad.

I threw off the beige comforter as goose bumps spread down my bare legs. Wearing only skivvies and a tank top, the cool morning chill made me reach for my robe sitting on a teal chair I had found at a thrift store and refurbished, along with a desk I had antiqued with white chalk paint. When you have no money, it's amazing the skills you can learn. The aroma of bacon wafted from the kitchen. I smiled, imagining tattooed, manly-man Tristan Cox wearing an apron over tighty-whities while flipping pancakes at the stove. Sliding into my Cookie Monster slippers—I was amazed to find my size—I headed for the kitchen where Tristan mixed scrambled eggs and cheese.

No tighty-whities like I had pictured, but just as sexy in his skin-hugging T-shirt and loose sweatpants that hung just low enough to make me drool. Or maybe I just really liked bacon.

"Need some help?" I offered as I grabbed the spatula and began tossing the strips of bacon—crispy but with little hillocks of fat around the edges, just like I liked it— onto an empty plate lined with a paper towel to soak up the grease.

"Hey, get back in bed. I wanted to surprise you." He grabbed my shoulders and attempted to guide me away from the stove that dated back to the 1980s, along with the rest of my outdated kitchen.

"How sweet of you," I purred, lifting on tiptoes to kiss his cheek. "But I'm already up." I could never fall back asleep once I stepped out of the warm cocoon of my comforter, no matter how long I toss and turn. "How about I set the table?"

The table was one foot away and consisted of my kitchen island.

Pulling two mismatched plates and different-sized coffee mugs from the cabinet, I placed the settings on the narrow periwinkle bar that separated the kitchen from the living room. My one-bedroom apartment wasn't much, but it was at least affordable on my meager salary filing paperwork at the Durham Police Department while I took criminal justice classes at Durham Tech. My dream was to become a professional private investigator, which required a license I could get only after I completed the coursework. But with a detective for a boyfriend and a job at the police station, I was on the fast track toward making it a reality. At least I hoped it was the fast track. I wasn't exactly a patient person.

"So what's on the agenda for the day? Kickin' ass and takin' names?" I asked as I poured us both coffee,

Tristan's black and in the smaller mug, mine more vanilla creamer than coffee in the larger one. If there was one thing I was selfish about, it was my coffee. I slid onto the wobbly bar stool and sipped the hot brew waiting for Tristan to join me. The chair leg tapped against the floor as I shifted in my seat.

"Oh, you know—the usual. Putting killers behind bars."

Tristan spooned eggs onto each of our plates, then added several pieces of just about perfect bacon. He fetched the pancakes from the stove—a short stack for me, a full stack for himself—and sat down next to me.

"Speaking of killers," he said, crunching noisily on his bacon, "what's up with Battan? Any updates on Marla Rivers?"

It was a case I couldn't shed. Many nights I found myself haunted by Marla's ghost, begging for me to help her. It wasn't that I was fascinated with the twelve-year-old girl's murder, but something compelled me to give her family the closure they deserved. Maybe it was our kindred suffering at such a young age, maybe it was my fear that my father was behind it, maybe it was a hunger for justice, or maybe it was just because I wanted to see George Battan fry. Whatever it was, I wanted Marla to be laid to rest—and that meant finding her killer.

"I was able to get Marla's case assigned to me, but until Tina's willing to testify that Marla was held captive with her in George's house, we don't have anything else to connect it to George—or anyone, for that matter. I'm guessing George wasn't holding the murder weapon, but I'm betting he hired whoever was. Until we can get more info from George, everyone's a suspect and no one's a suspect."

Tristan shook his head and forked eggs into his mouth. I suddenly felt too anxious to eat, but I took a bite anyway to show my appreciation for his effort.

"That poor family. I know how they feel—just wishing for closure. I felt the same way about Carli's death for over a decade, endlessly hoping for answers. No one deserves that kind of torment."

"Can you talk to Tina about it? Light a fire under her ass to speak up?"

Been there, done that. It was a conversation I'd had with Tina countless times, begging her to tell the police what she knew. She was the last person to see Marla alive as a fellow captive in George's child-trafficking hideaway. Before escaping, Tina had promised Marla she'd come back and rescue her, but that chance never came. Shortly after Tina fled, Marla's remains were found. The only reason Tina hadn't come forward with her information was because she needed leverage in order to get back her baby that George had stolen from her: Giana. Tina's plan was to use what she knew about Marla as a bargaining chip to force George to talk. Tell her where Giana was and she'd stay quiet about Marla. But George Battan wasn't known for playing fair, and I had a feeling Tina wouldn't end up winning at this mental chess match against him.

"I've tried talking to her, but she's determined to find Giana. She thinks keeping what she knows under wraps will get her what she wants."

Tristan forced a laugh. "Well, you can remind her that until she talks, all we have on George is a child sex trafficking charge—and that's not enough to keep him in prison for long. He'll be out with plenty of time to build a new life of crime. Is that what she wants?"

I shrugged, not sure how to answer that.

I pulled the stack of yesterday's mail on the counter toward me and began leafing through it. A bill. Several advertisements. Then a white envelope with my name handwritten across the front in neat, capitalized letters:

THE DEATH OF LIFE

Ari Wilburn

Sliding my finger across the top to tear it open, I found a single piece of plain white paper inside. I unfolded it and read the following message written with the same unnaturally clean script as the envelope:

Silence is your only salvation, or your family will pay for what they've done. I will be waiting and watching. They may think the past is buried, but I will unearth it all and drag them down to hell with me.

"What the hell ...?" I muttered, reading it a second time. As each word tunneled into my brain, my heart raced and my palms grew clammy. Fear clawed its way through me as worst-case scenarios played out in my mind's eye. Someone was targeting me ... intimately. Given there was no postage, the sender had physically dropped this letter in my mailbox. They had come to my home carrying a threat against me. They might have watched me through my windows. I might have even passed by them in the lobby. Had I brushed shoulders with this person bent on killing me? I could feel my face drain of warmth and color.

"What's wrong, babe?" Tristan glanced over at me, then followed my scared-stiff gaze. Silently reading the letter over my shoulder, he finally broke through my trance. "Put it down, Ari, in case I can get prints off this."

I felt his hand on my back, restoring me to the present. I carefully placed the paper on the counter. "Do you think George Battan is behind this?" If so, I was as good as dead. The man had ruthless henchmen everywhere.

"That's my best guess, considering you're the one who put him in jail. But I'm here, and I'll protect you. I won't let him or anyone else touch you, Ari. I promise." He pulled me into his arms, against his chest, almost suffocating me with his hug. But I didn't mind.

"You can't babysit me twenty-four hours a day, Tristan."

"Sure I can."

"But you don't live here. You have your own place."

"I could move in."

I shook my head and pulled back just enough to breathe. We hadn't even had the where-is-our-relationship-heading conversation yet. And now he wanted to move in ... so he could keep an eye on me? As much as I liked the thought of him always being around, I also hated the thought of him always being around. Cleaning up his dishes, washing his dirty underwear, sharing the remote control, wiping the golden droplets of pee off the toilet bowl rim—on those rare occasions when he'd remembered to flip the seat up. No, it was all too much too soon. There had to be another way to figure out what this threat meant, who it was from and why.

"No, that's not the answer. I need to find out what my father did, how he was connected to George. I don't think any of this crap will end until the truth all comes out."

The truth. If I was honest with myself, I feared the truth. I hid from the demon that kept watch over my parents, holding the people who raised me in its clutches. What atrocities had my father done in the name of "business"? What secrets had my mother harbored for him in the name of "family"? I shivered with a horrible feeling that the truth wouldn't just come back for my parents, but it would drown me with them.

Chapter 3
Ari

A grudge is like a snake in the grass. It slithers toward its target unseen, only the subtle movement of blades of grass tracking its path, until it rises from the earth and strikes, sinking its fangs into the flesh, paralyzing and then coiling around its prey until it's ready to dine. A grudge had been following me for about two weeks until it struck, and its prey was my best friend, Tina Alvarez.

We sat across from each other in a booth at Philly Steak—a hole-in-the-wall strip mall joint aptly named for having the best cheesesteak subs in the Triangle. With its aged yellow plastic booths and scuffed white ceramic floors it didn't look like much, but one taste of their tender steak smothered in provolone on a foot-long bun and you felt like you were in heaven. While Tina hungrily devoured her fries slathered in ketchup, I numbly stared at my food, too many angry thoughts in my head to enjoy it.

I never turned down a cheesesteak; Tina knew this about me.

Apparently my mood became obvious when she paused mid-chew to ask me, "What's going on in that pretty little head of yours?"

I glanced up. "What makes you think something's going on?"

"Duh. You're not eating one of your favorite foods on the planet. Normally you wouldn't come up for breath between bites. So ... what gives?"

I sighed. As well as Tina knew me, how did my frustration with her go unnoticed for so long? After two days of silent treatment, one-word text replies to her, and a begrudging lunch, I had expected her to catch on already and push for an explanation of my pissyness. Maybe I hadn't been bitchy enough, but it was time to come clean. "If you really wanna know, I'm pissed at you."

Her brown eyes rimmed in thick eyeliner widened in shock. "Pissed at me—why? What'd I do?"

"C'mon. Don't act dumb. We've talked about it a million times."

Leaning back, she crossed her arms and cracked her neck. The sound of popping joints made me wince. "Seriously? Is this about George Battan?"

"Yes!" I pounded the table with my fist, making my plate clatter and water tremble in my glass. "You're holding out on information that could put George Battan in prison for life. His trial is coming up, and all they have is a sex-trafficking charge, which is flaky at best. That gives him maybe a decade behind bars. He should be doing life, Tina. He ordered Marla's murder, and he deserves to pay for that. But no thanks to you, he won't be held accountable and Marla's family goes on mourning without justice."

She rolled her eyes at me, and the gesture reminded me that she was only eighteen years old. Still a kid. She had no clue how the real world worked, or that her choices had major consequences. I couldn't blame her for being so naïve. Despite this, I felt entitled to be mad about it because I wasn't that much older *or* wiser, and yet I still knew better.

"You know why I'm not talking. I need George to tell

me where Giana is. He won't talk unless I give him something—and that something is my silence about Marla and all the other girls."

"So that asshole promised to tell you where your baby is? He said those exact words?" I already knew the answer to my question. Tina hadn't even visited him in prison yet, and for good reason. The man had imprisoned her for years, tortured her, enslaved her to perform like a circus animal for sickos and perverts day after day. I knew why she couldn't face him yet, but to assume he'd cave to her demands was, well, just idiotic.

"Not exactly, but he will. Or else he'll be looking at death row when I tell everyone he killed Marla. I've got a royal flush, Ari. Relax. Marla's family will get closure ... after I get what I need. Unless you want me to drag your dad into it instead?"

"What did you just say?"

I couldn't believe she pulled the dad card on me. She knew I was trying to reconnect with my family, protect my parents, since I wasn't sure just how deep their involvement with George went. All I knew was that my good ol' daddy Burt Wilburn had ignited George's wrath fourteen years ago when George ordered a hit on my little sister Carli. What Burt had done to cause it, I'd never been able to pry out of him or my mom. The more I dug, the more they pushed me away. I had one clue that tied Dad to George, and it relied solely on Tina's memory. Three years ago my father took Tina's newborn baby away from her, and the only reason Tina hadn't turned him in yet was for my benefit.

"You know what, never mind," I grumbled. "I'll find a way to get in to talk to George and hopefully get something useful. I promised you I would help you find Giana and I'll follow through. Just don't bring my dad into it yet. Please?"

Her eyes passed over me, scrutinizing me like she was searching for the answer on my Nirvana T-shirt. "Deal … as long as you're buying dessert after this. Italian crème cake at Pomodoro's?" Her eyes twinkled.

I chuckled at how easy it was to sway Tina. The child in her could be bought with a Forever 21 outfit or Chinese takeout, but it made me wonder just how capable she was of being the parent in the scenario. Lots of mothers could feed a family on a waitress's wage, as long as they weren't blowing their slim earnings on shopping sprees and makeup. Tina couldn't stick to a budget if her life depended on it, yet she was going to keep a roof over Giana's head? I had my doubts.

"How can I say no to Italian crème cake? But you're in for a rude awakening once I find Giana. You'll be wearing Walmart mom jeans and eating generic mac 'n' cheese soon, girl."

"Uh, mom jeans are the new trend, Ari. Catch up. Besides, who says you can't be fashionable and a mom at the same time?"

Shaking my head, I realized Tina had no clue what she was in for as a parent. It wasn't like I knew much more, but at least I wasn't trying to become an instant parent of a three-year-old. The sacrifices, the hard work, the unconditional love—all values neither of us had been raised on.

The reality was, I didn't know what I was in for either, because finding Giana meant putting my father in jail, but no matter how much he hurt me as a child, he was still my dad. The same man I remembered carrying me on his shoulders at Durham Bulls baseball games, whose deep laughter shook a room, who acted out my bedtime stories using my stuffed animals, who joined me for tea parties. Once upon a time he was my hero. No matter what a man's done, a part of that hero lives on forever.

Save Giana or save my own father? It was a choice I could never make, but I might have to.

"So about finding Giana," I said, "tell me everything you remember about the day she was taken. Hopefully there's enough details that can lead me in the right direction for where to begin."

Tina's eyes misted as she turned away, as if facing the memory was too ugly. Looking somewhere beyond me, beyond the room, I watched as time took her back to the moment it happened three years ago.

"I remember it so well, yet I feel like I was a different person back then," she whispered.

In a way, she was. Three years ago she was still Sophia Alvarez, the abused victim. When she escaped she changed her name to Tina Alvarez, the survivor.

Her eyes glassy with tears, she continued, "All the perfect joy of meeting my daughter, and all the horrible pain of when she was stolen from me—every detail burned like a brand on my heart. It was the best thing and the worst thing that ever happened to me, all rolled into one sweet baby girl."

Chapter 4
Tina/Sophia Alvarez

Three years ago ...

It defied logic, the magic of childbirth. For eight hours fifteen-year-old Sophia Alvarez labored in agony, clutching her Hello Kitty bedsheets from when she had first arrived at the house nine years earlier, and screaming bloody murder as her body felt like it was ripping apart. The midwife George had hired with hush money coached Sophia through the birthing process, reminding her that pain meant progress, and to just keep breathing.

"Breathe through the contraction. Breathe through the pain."

But nothing helped take her mind off the tearing sensation as her muscles spasmed and abdomen cramped over and over in an endless cycle of torment. No breathing, no grunting, no groaning, no bath, no massage ... nothing eased the anguish as her body pooled with sweat and exhaustion sapped her endurance.

"Please take me to the hospital," Sophia cried.

"I'm sorry, honey, but I can't."

"I'm gonna die ... please help me."

But the answer remained a firm no.

During those eight excruciating hours Sophia begged to go to the hospital, begged for medicine, but her requests were denied. As the hours passed and her resolve weakened, she yearned for death, until that final push—the one that split her body in half—and then a head. A tiny body. Wriggling feet. And at last a baby's cries. Her baby's cries.

"It's a girl!" the midwife announced.

The miracle of birth was truly a miracle. One minute earlier Tina screamed for her life; the next minute she bathed in a warmth that stole all memory of it. Instantly the pain stopped and the enchantment took over as she watched her daughter enter her world. She'd never felt so alive and in love and at peace and overwhelmed with such joy in all of her short fifteen years of life. As the midwife handed the pink-faced baby to her, Sophia cradled the tiny, writhing creature in her arms, watching her delicate fingers wiggle and her bony toes curl. Everything about her daughter was perfect, from the cleft in her chin to the shock of black hair on her head. The baby's lips pursed in a suckling motion, then a moment later widened as she belted out a scream Sophia hadn't expected from something so small.

"I think she's hungry," Sophia said, appealing to the midwife for help.

The midwife nodded. "I think you're right, honey."

The midwife turned to leave, and as the baby continued to wail, Sophia began to grow frantic. But then the magic returned, and somehow, even without her mama there to teach her the ways of motherhood, Sophia's maternal instinct took over and she pressed the baby to her breast and helped her latch. The cries immediately ended as the baby nursed, until the midwife stepped into the room. Pulling the baby away, she shook her head.

"No, dear, no nursing. Here, give her a bottle."

The midwife handed Sophia a warm bottle of formula,

and Sophia placed the nipple on the baby's tongue. She squirmed and pushed the plastic out of her mouth with her tongue, scrunching her face in disgust.

"She doesn't want it. What should I do?"

"It takes getting used to. Just keep trying."

The midwife watched on as Sophia offered the bottle, and after several minutes of back-and-forth negotiations, the baby finally accepted the drink and quieted down.

"I love her so much. I want to name her Giana. It means 'God is gracious.' Isn't that a perfect name for her?"

The midwife rested her hand on Sophia's shoulder. "It's beautiful. You did so great, Sophia." A moment later she hustled out of the room, leaving Sophia alone with Giana in fairy-tale bliss.

But the happily-ever-afterglow didn't last long. It wasn't meant to last, but no one had told Sophia. For a month Sophia bonded with Giana, eagerly tending to her midnight feedings, singing silly songs while she changed dirty diapers. She floated through life like in a dream, and it wasn't so bad. Until it took a drastic turn for the worse.

The nattering of a preternaturally cheerful afternoon TV talk show host had lulled Sophia to sleep in the living room with Giana tucked into the crook of her arm. Skin to skin, mother and babe had been slumbering deeply when the midwife returned. When Sophia felt the weight and warmth of the baby lift from her, she awoke to the midwife hovering over her, offering soothing instructions to stay put, she was just putting the baby down in her crib to do her monthly checkup. Nothing unusual, as the midwife had stopped by several times to check on the baby and Sophia's healing progress. But it wasn't a checkup like Sophia had been told.

It was a kidnapping ploy.

Minutes later George and a mustached man she had never seen before barged through the front door and stormed into the baby's room.

As the midwife handed the baby to the mysterious man, she said, "Sophia suggested Giana for a name. I think it suits her."

"I didn't ask for your opinion," George spat back. He turned to Mustache Man. "Did you get the payment in full?"

Mustache Man nodded, handing a black duffel bag to George, who set it against the wall. "All cash, every dollar counted and recorded. The family understands the terms. They're pretty desperate to do anything for this. Several legal adoptions already fell through, so they're happy to skip the red tape. I think we're all set."

"Alright, then let's do this." George turned and briskly left the bedroom with Mustache Man, holding the baby, close behind.

The wheels began cranking inside Sophia's head. Something was wrong.

"Hey, where are you taking Giana?" Sophia called out, scrambling to her feet.

The midwife thrust out her arm to stop her, but Sophia plowed through, now in a run. She stopped short of the entryway as George and Mustache Man spoke in low tones. Sophia had a horrible foreboding, but she couldn't figure out why.

"How's the baby look? I don't want any problems before everything goes through."

"Everything looks perfect, sir," came the midwife's voice from behind Sophia.

"Can I please have Giana back?" Sophia asked with force.

She reached out her hands and stepped forward, but George roughly pushed her backward. "She's not your baby, Sophia. Go back to your room."

"What are you talking about? You can't just take my

daughter away from me."

"And what will you do to stop me?" George's lips curled into a cruel smirk. "I own you, child. Your parents sold you to me, remember? You have no one but me. You would die without me—I'd make sure of it. So learn your place, or I will teach you the hard way." He turned to Mustache Man. "As for the baby, you know what to do. Take care of it."

"No, you can't do this!" Sophia screamed hysterically. A fierce beast within Sophia awakened as she watched her baby being taken away forever. Claws bared, she lunged at Mustache Man, gouging four deep furrows in his cheek. Mustache Man cursed and flung her to the floor. George leapt on top of her, pinning her shoulders down with his knees.

"Knock it off, bitch!" The vicious backhand to her cheek only increased her protective fury.

"Give me my baby!" she shrieked, writhing her arms free.

Again George lifted his hand to strike her, this time with his clenched fist. Covering her face with her arms, she deflected his punch, then clawed at his eyes. But his glasses took the brunt of the assault, giving him just enough time to wrap his hands around her throat, suffocating her cries as he squeezed.

"Burt, go!" George ordered the Mustache Man. His footsteps clattered across the wooden floor. A moment later Sophia heard the front door slam shut, closing on any hope she had of getting her daughter back.

George pressed his face close, his breath fluttering Sophia's hair. "This is your final warning. If you dare try to leave, I will make sure your baby dies. The best thing you can do to protect her is to listen to me. She will be with a good family, not some punk-ass teenage whore like you. If you know what's good for you—and for the baby—

you'll calm down, go to your room, and heal up so that we can get you back to work. You've had enough time off already. Got it?"

Her nod was barely perceptible with the pressure of his hands on her throat, but it was enough of an affirmation that he released her. She coughed explosively as she twisted away from him, shuffling toward the wall. When she finally caught her breath, she looked up to find herself alone in the room, except for the movement of a shadow. Glancing up, she met the eyes of the midwife, who gazed sadly down at Sophia.

"I'm sorry, honey."

With those last words Sophia never saw the midwife, or her baby girl, again.

Chapter 5

Ari

SILENCE IS YOUR ONLY SALVATION, OR YOUR FAMILY WILL PAY FOR WHAT THEY'VE DONE. I WILL BE WAITING AND WATCHING. THEY MAY THINK THE PAST IS BURIED, BUT I WILL UNEARTH IT ALL AND DRAG THEM DOWN TO HELL WITH ME.

A shiver coursed down my spine as I examined the note on my office desk, now encased in a gallon-sized plastic evidence bag that Tristan had provided. For the past day I could think of nothing else but whoever was behind the threat and what exactly it meant. My first guess was George Battan because of his upcoming trial in which I would be testifying. My testimony would most likely mean a death sentence for me, courtesy of Battan.

Yet a sliver of doubt remained: what if it wasn't him? If this stalker knew anything about my family history, certainly they should know I hadn't been part of my parents' lies—or lives—since I was ten years old and thrown into the foster care system. If anything, I was more clueless to their hidden life than anyone, especially this bastard threatening me. So why come after me? What could I possibly do—or know—that would give this scumbag what he wanted ... that is, if he wanted something.

I could draw only one conclusion. *Silence was my salvation*—it had to be a warning that I shouldn't testify. Which meant it had to be George Battan ... right?

Then why wasn't I so sure?

My computer screensaver swirled a rainbow of colors as I pushed the note aside and shook my head at the yellow stack of case files I needed to organize. While I loved working as a filing clerk at the Durham Police Department, overhearing confidential intel on various cases, and learning about the investigation techniques, the administrative aspects sucked monkey balls, especially after eight hours stuck in a stuffy, claustrophobic filing room or updating notes in the system until my fingertips went numb. But it was better than flipping burgers or cleaning out department store dressing rooms, so I couldn't complain ... aloud, at least.

I felt movement behind me, and suspecting it was my boss, I hurriedly slid the note under a folder while hitting a key on my keyboard to bring my computer to life so I'd look busy.

"I won't tell on you," a sexy voice whispered in my ear as strong hands squeezed my shoulders. "You're lucky I like having you around here."

I exhaled relief. It was Tristan, not the creepy police cadet who'd been trying to get in my pants since I got hired. "You scared the shit out of me. Why's the captain always gotta be hovering when I'm not working?"

"If you didn't do your little side projects at work, you wouldn't get caught, babe."

I gazed up at him as he looked down at me. From his upside-down view his grin looked comically large.

"Side projects keep me sane. Speaking of, got any delicious crime crumbs for me? Any clues you want me to follow up on?" I flashed an exaggerated hopeful smile, already knowing the answer. It was a dance we'd choreographed to perfection. I'd beg for real police work, he'd turn me down, and I'd eventually persuade him to disclose something, anything, which I'd chew on until my shift ended.

"Aw, my murder-obsessed girlfriend. So cute. And comforting for me." He raised an eyebrow skeptically. "But no, no new leads on any cases." I watched his eyes wander to the threatening message peeking out from under my to-file pile. "You still worried about that?"

"Nah. I'll find out who sent it and make him cot-mates with George Battan in jail."

But the truth was I was terrified. I'd spent a lifetime hiding my fear, stuffing it down deep beneath my skin until I was calloused from all emotions. At least I thought I was. But no matter how hard you try to suppress your human nature, there's always a trigger that will waken your true self. I'd played tough girl for fourteen years, and I was well practiced at it, but the act only lasted so long. Today, however, I was giving my best performance.

"So you're okay?" Tristan probed again.

"Yeah, I swear. I just want to figure out who sent it and what they want. Do you think it's George, sending a message through his cronies?" I felt like I was in the cast of *The Sopranos* dealing with wiseguys and goons.

"That's the most likely person to send this, especially with the trial coming up. But then again, I don't know how many other enemies your father has, or what other motives George would have to off you."

"How much time do you have?" Tristan moved to my side as I spoke. "I'm wondering if he knows Tina remembers Marla. He's got to have pieced that together by now. But if that was the case, wouldn't he be sending a threat to Tina too?"

Tristan sighed with a shrug. "I can't predict the inner workings of a psychopathic child molester. I'm gonna regret suggesting this, but maybe we could talk to him."

"We—as in you and me?" I couldn't believe he was cool with taking me into the prison to visit the man who nearly killed me once before, and seemed set on going another round.

"Don't get too excited. I just want to see how he reacts or what he knows. But that's not what I came over here to talk to you about. Got a minute?" Before I could answer, he rolled up a chair from the empty cubicle next to mine and sat.

"What's up?"

"You know that murder case I told you about, the one that might involve a serial killer?"

Of course I remembered. I lived for those conversations over Mellow Mushroom pizza together, when Tristan unloaded his work stress on my eager ears. Finding and catching villains was my new passion, and I absorbed everything I learned like a tick on a hound. The case involved two victims—that Tristan knew of—both with the same *modus operandi*. While the link between them wasn't certain, Tristan had a hunch, and his hunches were usually right.

Like when he had a hunch that I started stress smoking shortly after I got hired at the precinct, thanks to Tristan's recommendation. Maybe it was the cigarette smoke clinging to my clothes, or the frequent "bathroom breaks" that gave me away, but two days in he confronted me with a "hunch" that I was smoking—and hiding it. He didn't care so much about the habit, just that I was lying about it.

Lying felt a bit extreme to describe my secret. *Nondisclosure* would have been the word I used. Tomayto, tomahto, I didn't want to escalate the debate over it, so I admitted the truth, although the vulnerability felt damn scary. Truth be told, I was petrified of screwing up, of letting him down, and smoking helped calm my frenzied nerves. I'd finally landed a decent job in a field I loved, the criminal justice classes were a huge step toward my private investigator future, and my life for once didn't look so bleak. I had something to lose, and knowing Life's penchant for trickery, like biting into a chocolate cake only to discover it's pumpernickel, everything good would slip through my fingers at any moment. So I smoked the fear away.

Tristan had hugged me then, kissed my forehead like a father comforting a daughter. And I almost shed a tear at the intimacy of that moment—almost. But private investigators couldn't dissolve into a mess of emotions, could they, so I swallowed the feelings down and laughed at myself instead. That's when I noticed that Tristan hadn't laughed with me, but instead held me with an acceptance of who I was, how I ticked.

No more secrets, I had promised him that day. And I walked away from our first boyfriend/girlfriend fight happier than I'd ever been, because I had someone who gave a shit about my secrets.

"Yeah, the killer you think might be connected to the suicide support group," I answered. "Did you find a lead?"

"Possibly." Tristan scratched his goatee with a chewed fingernail. "I did more digging. Found some interesting stuff."

Ooh, I loved *stuff.*

The cases had turned cold after weeks of no leads and other, fresher cases to pursue. Their priority had dwindled for everyone but Tristan. The media attention hadn't lasted long. When victims were a woman or child, it was heartbreaking news. When they were men, however, it didn't tug on the heartstrings so much.

The first victim, three months ago, was Scott Guffrey, found dead in his living room, his neck sliced open. The toxicology report came back showing excessive alcohol consumption and the presence of flunitrazepam—better known as the date rate drug or a roofie, street slang derived from the psychoactive drug's more common name, Rohypnol. His ex-girlfriend and neighbors had nothing but good things to say about him, couldn't imagine who would want to kill an upstanding fellow who always helped anyone in need. Of course, such sentiments were always so gushing postmortem, since rarely did anyone say the victim was a complete asshat and deserved what he got. Scott's list of enemies and motives for murder was short—more like nonexistent. Father of two kids and dedicated employee at Drew's Plumbing, the man never missed work or his son's baseball games. On paper he was father of the year. In reality he did something to get himself killed, and I desperately wanted to help Tristan find out what.

Victim number two was Jackson Jones, found dead in his car, also with his throat slit open, one month ago. Similar method of death, but different locale and about two months apart. Except this time no alcohol, no date rape drugs. Perhaps the killer was warming up with Scott before targeting Jackson and needed Scott pliable. But Jackson being a target made just as little sense. A dedicated husband, reliable employee, with a gorgeous home, and married but no kids, Jackson was a shocking choice of victim. Worked in the IT department at the Social Services office. No apparent enemies, no indiscretions that Tristan could uncover. And no apparent ties to Scott, which made me wonder what secrets they shared that made them both a target.

It wasn't a guarantee that the same killer took them both out, except for one seemingly indifferent detail: they both had a connection to my suicide support group. Scott had a flyer for the Triad Suicide Support Group (not the most clever or original name, I admit) on his dining room table. Jackson had been on his way home from his first meeting when he was murdered. I vaguely recalled him; he hadn't spoken much, just briefly introduced himself as Joe and observed the group, then left in a hurry. It was an almost indiscernible connection between the victims, but it was still there.

Coincidence or not, it made me wonder if the threat I'd gotten wasn't from George after all, but from the person who killed Scott and Jackson. Was I the common thread?

"What kind of stuff?" I asked.

"From outward appearance the victims seem randomly selected. Both have no prior records, enviable family lives, no questionable affiliations. Except when I started looking into Scott's medical history, I found that he was prescribed an anti-depressant just under two years ago. Normally that wouldn't be a red flag, but it led me to wonder what happened two years ago that might have caused him to spiral into depression. Then I discover Scott had been living with a woman named Helen Brannigan. In fact, they were engaged to get married. Guess what happened two years ago?"

I shrugged and shook my head. "You got me. What?"

"Helen's five-year-old daughter, Kat Brannigan, was abducted from their home. Body never turned up. Still an open missing persons case, but we're assuming she's dead. Scott had an airtight alibi and wasn't a suspect, but what if his killer was behind Kat's murder as well?"

"An interesting theory, but Jackson doesn't fit into it."

"Not that we know … yet. I have a gut feeling this is all connected somehow—Kat's abduction, Scott's death, and Jackson's part of it somehow, I'm sure. What do you think? Am I crazy?"

I loved how Tristan respected me enough to ask my opinion.

"I think you're on to something. If that is the case, it'd

be nice to give the Brannigans closure after all this time wondering about their daughter." I knew how they felt. I had lived with fourteen years of wondering who was behind the wheel that killed my sister. Sure, it hurts to know, but I think it hurts worse not to know. "So all we gotta do is find Scott's killer and save the day. Easy peasy." I flashed Tristan a goofy smile. "Where do we start?"

"*We*? There's no *we* in this, Ari. You know you can't be investigating this until you get your license."

"Sure, sure ..." I mumbled.

Oh, how much Tristan still had to learn about me. You couldn't hide a bone this tasty and not expect me to dig for it. It was either obsess over the threatening note or focus my energy on finding Scott and Jackson's killer.

"You promise to stay out of it?" Tristan cupped my chin and forced me to meet his eyes. I couldn't look away from those penetrating baby blues of his; they were my kryptonite. "Ari?"

"Fine," I grumbled. "I'll try my best not to."

But like I said, Tristan had so much left to learn about me. I wasn't the best at staying out of trouble.

Chapter 6
Ari

One month ago ...

"What are you in for?"

Jackson Jones glanced over at me from his stiff seat next to mine. The ring of gray metal folding chairs was still half-empty as people lingered by the snack table covered with cookies and generic bottles of soda, waiting for the suicide support group meeting to begin.

"Excuse me?" he asked, his forehead wrinkling with confusion.

"Just a joke. I was asking why you were here." With his clean-shaven jaw, neatly combed hair, collared polo shirt, and khaki slacks, the man oozed all work and no play. A perfect recipe for suicide, in my opinion. Dressed like an accountant, I imagined him carefully ironing his pants then standing before his bathroom mirror while slicking down his hair, the routine a pleasant-looking mask for the horror that lived inside of him.

I figured he would feel more comfortable sharing if I told my story first, so I plodded ahead, weaving the lie as I went along. "I'm here because I tried to hang myself. I've been struggling with ... urges ... that I can't control. That whole *take one day at a time* mantra, well, it's harder than it sounds."

I paused, hoping he'd jump in at any time. When he didn't, I continued rambling. "It's hopeless, you know? I want to stop feeling this way, but I'm broken. Killing myself seemed like the only way out. But here I am, trying to stop death from being the only option."

Jackson watched me with skeptical eyes. I couldn't tell if it he bought the act or saw right through me. Maybe he saw a little of himself in me.

"Yeah, I get it. I've only thought about it—suicide, that is—but never acted on it. Honestly, I'm not sure why I'm here other than to get perspective, I guess."

But I knew why he was here. To be honest, I was surprised that this was where he led me as I followed him, two cars behind, from his work. I didn't take him for feeling guilty about his secrets. Scared of getting caught, yes. But remorse, no. Regardless of why he was here, he was a monster that needed to be wiped off the face of the earth. If not by his own hand, then by mine.

I introduced myself with a fake name, waiting for a polite exchange.

"I'm Joe," he replied. Another liar like me.

"This seat taken?" On the other side of me stood a woman with long, silky raven hair, parted in the middle and ironing-board straight. She reminded me of Morticia Addams, but the blue eyes on her pale, oval face were intelligent and friendly—and she wore jeans and blouse from the Gap, not a hobble-skirted dress with octopus tentacles at the hem.

"Nope, it's all yours."

She extended her hand to me as she sat and I shook it. "Destiny Childs. Suicide survivor. Though I lost a daughter to it. You're new, right?"

I nodded. "Yep, first time here."

"Nervous?"

"Not really."

"It can be overwhelming at first, y'know, sharing your history, your pain. But I'll tell you, it's healing. It helped me work through a lot of crap after losing Clarissa, finding peace and acceptance of what happened. We can't change the past, but we can shape the future."

She sounded like a walking billboard for the group, but I didn't want to offend her, so I smiled instead.

"I hope that's true. I guess that's why I'm here—to shape the future. Make it better."

She touched my shoulder lightly. "Good for you."

Yes, good for me and the rest of society. But not so good for Jackson—I mean *Joe*.

Jackson Jones had been quiet after his initial vague introduction, fidgeting in his seat and glancing at the clock every few minutes. As soon as the hour-long session was over, he rushed out the large glass double doors of the church where the meetings were held like he was on fire. I knew the truth, though. I knew the darkness that clawed its way out of him, peeling off his morality like a snake shedding its skin.

I followed closely behind. A bright streetlight bathed the parking lot in harsh white. All the other members of the group had remained inside for fellowship and refreshments.

"Hey, Joe," I called out. By now he had stopped at his car door and was unlocking it.

At first he attempted to ignore me—or didn't recognize the fake name he'd used—so I yelled louder. "Joe, right?"

This time he looked up as he opened his car door. "Yeah?"

"Any chance you're heading near Oleander Way?" I knew the uppity neighborhood was where he lived, so he'd be lying if he said no. Plus someone who lived on Oleander Way certainly wouldn't have the need to rob him, if that's what he was worried about.

"Uhh ..." Jackson faltered, glanced away from me into the darkness that began to shroud us.

I waited a beat, then added, "My friend dropped me off and is borrowing my car, but I can't seem to reach him now. I was hoping to hitch a ride home, if it's not out of your way. If it's a problem, no biggie. I can see if anyone else is driving that way. Or just wait until my friend comes to get me." I added the last part as an extra guilt trip.

He exhaled, turned to me, then nodded toward the car. "Oleander Way, you said? Yeah. Alright. Get in. I'll drop you off."

"Thank you so much. I appreciate this." I ran around to the passenger side door and hopped in.

After giving him a fake address three doors down from where he lived, my heart drummed the whole way there. Lucky for me Jackson kept to himself and didn't know that a Ms. Eller, a wealthy dowager, actually lived there.

Despite the risk of taking him out virtually in his front yard, I wanted him close to home when his dead body was discovered; I wanted his wife to find the beast she married put down like an animal. It was poetic justice that the man who brought evil into his home died in his own hoity-toity neighborhood.

Not a soul was about as Jackson piloted his whisper-quiet Lexus through the empty streets. Sweat beaded on my lip and I soaked it up with my sleeve. The adrenalin rush—anticipation of the kill—was both intoxicating and sobering.

As he pulled up to the curb, I unbuckled my seatbelt then slid my hand into my jeans pocket, feeling for the familiar slickness of the utility knife's handle. Cool in my clammy palm, I gripped it tightly and pulled out the blade, resting the razor edge against my outer thigh as Jackson parked the car.

"Thanks again, Jackson," I said, only a moment too

late realizing my slipup. Unfortunately, Jackson noticed it too.

"How do you know my real name?" His voice was gravelly with anger and he turned to me with a hard stare.

I couldn't waste another moment. Lunging across the seat, I jammed the index finger and thumb of my left hand into his eye sockets and squeezed. He flailed his arms and screamed girlishly as my knife hand sought his neck. A random blow sent me flying against the passenger-side window. For an infinitesimal moment I saw the raw terror in his eyes before I bounced back at him. With a feral cry I pulled the short blade across the bastard's neck with a satisfying *snik*. A bright red necklace sprouted on his throat, where the Adam's apple rose and fell convulsively. I felt my fingers lace around my own neck sympathetically. In the rearview mirror I glimpsed my avid expression and wicked grin.

His cries ceased almost immediately, drowning into a bubbly gurgle.

"Why?" he rasped. The word was short and wet, a final question that the world would never answer. Blood soaked the collar of his Eton shirt as he slumped against the door, his eyelids fluttering then closing.

Although veiled by evening on an empty street, I felt the urgency to get the hell out of Dodge. I needed only a minute more to clean up after my mess. In my back pocket I had brought alcohol pads to wipe away my fingerprints. Ripping open a packet, I ran the alcohol pad over Jackson's eyes, then pulled my sleeve over my hand and opened the door, swiping the cloth over the handles inside and out. I'd worn all black to mask any blood spatter, but I couldn't help but break into a jog to put as much distance between me and Jackson as quickly as possible. Only when I found myself two blocks over did I finally slow my pace, and that's when I hit the wall of regret.

I'd just killed another person. A human being.

I didn't even give him a chance to say goodbye to his wife or to explain why he did what he did.

I was becoming just like the monsters I loathed.

And yet I suddenly felt unstoppable.

Chapter 7
Ari

If I were to imagine millions of tiny, hairy spiders crawling all over my skin, that's what it felt like the moment I saw him: George Battan, his wire-rimmed glasses slipping down his sweaty nose, dwarfed in a faded orange jumpsuit, being led into the visitor's room by a mammoth black guard. The man's boxy shaved head sat on the stump of his neck, forming a single ebony monolith. His V-shaped torso tapered down to a slim waist. Admiring his python arms, I pictured him snapping George Battan's swizzle stick body in half over one of his tree trunk legs. The guard caught me smiling. I looked guiltily away from his flinty stare.

"Fifteen minutes, Battan." The basso profundo voice reeked with unquestioned authority.

Battan's chair squealed as it scraped against the concrete floor. A cool metal table connected us, while a wall-to-wall piece of Plexiglas kept him safely tucked away where I couldn't strangle him. I bit back the urge to drive my fist through the plastic and wipe the shit-eating grin off his smug face.

Two chairs down from me a young mother holding her infant son played peek-a-boo with Daddy through the glass. Despite the miasma of violence and animalistic survival that permeated the place, the family laughed as if the world around them had melted away and it was just them enjoying family time in their living room.

I felt oddly at home in this cinderblock shell, probably from years of growing up in the foster system and being shuffled from facility to facility. Hostile and sterile, it represented my view of the world, of my heart. But Tristan was slowly, steadily chipping away the rough edges, reviving every part of me, even parts I didn't know I had.

George picked up the phone on his side; I followed suit. "Ari Wilburn. Slumming in the ol' slammer, are we? I hope you didn't come empty-handed." George leaned forward and folded his thin arms on the table with a casualness that annoyed me. The man was in jail and he acted like we were chatting over breakfast at the Waffle House.

The scent of betrayal wafted over me; I hoped Tristan would forgive me for my secret visit without him today, but it was something I needed to do on my own. I didn't want him there no matter how much he felt he needed to protect me. At breakfast this morning I had forgotten to mention that I planned to visit Battan. Well, maybe *forgotten* wasn't the right word. A simple omission. I'd tell him after the fact. It was easier to ask for forgiveness than to ask for permission, not that I needed his permission. I was a grown-ass woman, for crying out loud. I was allowed to visit an inmate if I wanted to ... even though this inmate happened to be the one I would be testifying against soon. I made sure not to mention that when I requested the visit.

"I'm here on business, so don't get too excited. And it's not being recorded, in case you were wondering."

"When they told me I had a visitor, I never imagined it would be you. I almost didn't believe them. I didn't expect you to care so much. But this is a nice treat."

"Yeah, well, I'm not here to stroke your ego or retract

my testimony, in case you were hoping."

"No pleasantries? Oh Ari, you're no fun. Always one to cut to the chase."

"Look, I don't want to be here any more than you want to see me. But we've run into a … situation. One that we could maybe help each other with."

He leaned back, arms still folded, eyes narrowing on me. Those beady eyes made my skin crawl. "I'm listening."

"Right now you're only facing maybe seven to ten years for child sex trafficking. And with good behavior, they might offer you early parole. But what if I told you I had evidence you killed Marla Rivers that could put you behind bars for life?"

"I'd say you're bluffing," he sniffed. But the sudden sickly pallor of his face told me much more.

"Is that a risk you're willing to take?"

"You said this was a situation we could help each other with. This doesn't sound like you're helping me at all." He massaged his face with surprisingly long and elegant hands, restoring the pink color. His cool demeanor unsettled me. I was dancing with the devil.

"Here's where that comes into play. You know who has Giana Alvarez, Tina's baby. Give me a name and I'll see what I can do to keep murder off your rap sheet."

"Considering I know you don't have evidence on me, this isn't a deal, Ari. This is child's play. You're not ready for the big leagues, little girl. Are we done now?"

I couldn't give up so easily. "George, please. What do you have to lose by giving me a name?"

Battan made a strange hooting in his throat that made me sit back in my chair. The sound exploded into raucous cackling, like the crazy vocalizations of a barred owl that, as a little girl, I'd heard one night outside the bedroom window of one of my many foster homes. It took me a moment to realize he was laughing. Even the hulking black guard seemed dismayed and shuffled his feet a little nervously, I thought.

"Oh, you have so much to learn. You should know by now that I don't fold when I have a winning hand."

"But you did kill Marla, and I *will* prove it."

He leaned forward, pointing his finger and resting the tip against the glass. "Just remember what you're threatening, Ari. If you try to pin that on me, you're taking your father down with me. Is that what you want? To put your own flesh and blood behind bars for life ... or worse? They don't take too kindly to child killers in these parts." His breath left a frosty film on the windowpane.

The guard approached from behind George, lifting him by his shoulders from his seat like a doll.

"Quit your jibba jabba, Battan. Time to go."

Before backing away, he pointed at me. Then with his fingertip he wrote in the condensation that still clung to the glass, the digit sliding across the surface like he relished every second of my suspense as each letter was painstakingly formed, backward from his perspective, readable from mine:

DIE, ARI.

"Is that a threat, asshole?" I yelled back at him, slamming my fist against the Plexiglas, my cheeks burning. The guard shot me a warning look.

George snickered, pleased he'd riled me. "No, Ari, what you got in the mail—now *that's* a threat."

Chapter 8
Ari

Child Trafficker Linked to Murder

Durham, North Carolina

In addition to facing child trafficking charges filed last month, George Battan has been indicted for the murder of Marla Rivers, the ten-year-old daughter of Bill and Justine Rivers. After going missing December 6, 2013, Rivers' remains were recovered in Eno River Park on June 8, 2015, when a hiker stumbled upon a shallow grave. Dental records confirmed the skeletal remains were those of the missing child.

"I had always hoped Marla was out there somewhere, alive," a grieving Justine Rivers commented. "At least now I can lay my baby girl to rest."

After almost a year of no leads, the Durham Police Department received a tip that Battan was behind the murder. According to an anonymous eyewitness testimony, Rivers had been held hostage by Battan at a Durham residence and forced into a child prostitution ring. Investigators are currently looking into the authenticity of the claims.

Burt Wilburn, manager of SunTrust Bank Durham branch, was later brought in for questioning, although the nature of his involvement is undisclosed. Investigators are currently pursuing all leads that could give closure to the Rivers family.

"All we want is whoever killed Marla to get what they deserve," Bill Rivers told the press in an interview yesterday. "A murderer is still on the loose, and we intend to do whatever it takes to stop him from making another family go through the pain that we've gone through."

Any additional information should be reported to the Durham Police Department.

As I read the article in the *News & Observer* on my back porch that afternoon, I saw red. Tina, *you friggin' idiot, what the hell were you thinking?* By incriminating Battan and mentioning my father, she was leading the cops straight to my father's door, when really what did she know? A vague memory of a mustached man who may or may not have been my father taking Giana from her over three years ago. How could she be so sure it was Burt? Lots of guys had mustaches ...

Despite what my dad had done to me, giving up on me,

tossing me to the wolves as a child, he was still my father. My flesh. My blood. My memories. The one who kissed my skinned knee after I had fallen off my bike. The one who carried me on his shoulders at the zoo so I could see the lions, tigers, and bears, oh my. The one who taught me to body surf the waves during day trips to Wrightsville Beach. Although the years had faded my memories to gray, I couldn't step aside while my father took the heat for Battan's crimes ... not until I knew the truth.

People of power and means like Battan had their ways of throwing others under the bus. I couldn't let my father be his scapegoat while Battan got a slap on the wrist. Now that Tina leaked this to the press, it'd be an uphill battle to cover it back up, pack it down, until I could find out exactly how my father was involved. In the meantime, Tina would be getting an earful from me about it.

It was a North Carolinian late spring, the brief balmy season between when the winter chill drove you indoors to seek warmth and the summer heat drove you indoors to the air conditioning. For a few precious weeks I could sit on my porch in shorts and a T-shirt without sweating myself damp in minutes. I wanted to enjoy the woods-scented breeze, the song of the whip-poor-will, the sprouts of color lining the concrete walkways.

And yet Tina, in her passive-aggressive way, managed to ruin it for me. While the tulip poplars were in full majestic bloom, adorned with orange and yellow flowers, and tiny vetch blossoms carpeted the earth in purple, all I felt was angry red.

I pushed the pile of lacy bras, skinny jeans, and strappy tank tops from the torn love seat cushion to the floor. Tina's thick mascara rimmed her eyes like she'd slept in it, and her dark roots poking out beneath her at-home blond dye job were a loud cry for a trip to the hairdresser.

A hidden bag of Doritos Cool Ranch chips crunched and crackled under my butt as I sat down in a pile of crumbs.

"Don't you ever clean up? This place is a dump." I grimaced at the stench of rotting Chinese takeout and stale pizza. I moved an empty mug aside, unsticking it from the cheap Ollie's coffee table I'd bought her, leaving a brown tacky ring of what I assumed had been coffee once upon a time.

"I wasn't expecting company." Tina lifted her shoulders and stacked some dishes, then carried the filthy heap to the kitchen, where she'd managed to fit a small table and two chairs into one corner. It was the only open space to eat at, now that her dining room table was covered in shopping bags, furniture store advertisements, and more dirty dishes. I wondered why a single woman needed twenty place settings when she clearly wasn't hosting dinner parties.

After dumping the dishes on the marbled gray countertop, she returned and sat next to me. "Better?"

I eyed the dirty laundry strewn across the carpet, the mail littering the floor, the food stains on the sofa, the trash scattered throughout the room. How could she live like this? Worse yet, how did she expect to raise a child in this? But that wasn't my call to make, was it?

"Sure, I guess." I handed her the crumpled bag of chips, which she tossed on the coffee table, spilling the remainder of its contents. "I need to talk to you about something."

"What's up?"

Sitting cross-legged on the sofa next to me, she stretched; I caught the sparkle of the purple navel ring peeking out from under her shirt. The bauble was a tacky vestige of Tina's sexual exploitation; I marveled that she hadn't had it removed, but then, in many ways, she was a coarse girl, guarded and even a little strange. Who wouldn't be, after all the shit she'd been through? The needle-phobic in me wondered how much it hurt and why anyone would consent to having a needle jabbed through their flesh in a vain attempt to look "sexy." A senseless trauma, if you asked me, but then again, I'd rather suffer three weeks with the flu than get a one-second prick of a flu shot.

"I have a bone to pick with you. You told the press about George Battan's connection to Marla's murder. And now my dad was brought in for questioning."

"So? What's the big deal?"

"Are you seriously asking me that right now? You know my father is probably connected, and if he talks he's as good as dead. If he doesn't talk, the police will keep coming at him."

"Maybe he's getting what he deserves. Have you ever considered that? Besides, if he's innocent, you don't need to worry."

She had me there. But no matter what sense of justice Tina tied to her actions, it still stung like a betrayal.

"It doesn't always work that way. What really upsets me is that instead of talking to me first, you go behind my back—while I'm trying to help you find Giana, by the way—and you basically incriminate my father. Why would you do that while I'm trying to help you?"

"Ari, you couldn't possibly understand."

She was right. I would never understand, because she lost both of her parents in a matter of weeks and didn't flinch, didn't mourn the loss, handled it with an emotional buoyancy that would make Hannibal Lecter proud. While I clung to whatever hope remained that I'd be reunited with my family, she dismissed hers with a shrug. Even though we shared the trauma of being castaways, the impact that heartbreak made on each of us couldn't be more different. I grew more desperate to fix my family while Tina reupholstered her heart with leather.

"I already knew George wasn't going to talk," she continued in a defensive bluster. "I was raised by him. Don't you think I know him by now? Your dad was already screwed. George would've brought him down without my help. I'm trying to get answers, and the only way to do that is to light a fire under both their asses."

"You don't know that Battan won't talk. I saw him— and he's nervous. He knows he's caught."

"Okay, miss know-it-all. Tell me, what information did you get about Giana?"

Damn. I couldn't deny the truth that I walked out as empty-handed as when I had arrived. "Nothing yet, but I will."

"Whatever. You don't know him like I do. He'll never give me what I need to know because that's what he does: holds out a carrot while beating you with a stick. Only so you can discover there was no carrot after all. He's an illusionist, Ari. Always a trick. I had to do what I had to do to motivate him. Now he knows I'm serious."

"Yeah, well, you should have talked to me first. I'm doing all of this for you, and now he'll know I was bluffing because the police have nothing on him but your word against his. And I hate to remind you, but George has a way of disposing of people who speak up against him. I don't want to be reading about your 'deadly accident' in the news next week."

Rising from the sofa, Tina walked to the kitchen, grabbed a soda from the fridge, and returned to stand at the edge of the living room.

"I wish you'd be honest with yourself, Ari. This isn't

about me or Giana; it's about you. About restoring your family. I get it. I do. That's why I want my daughter back. But don't pretend this is some chess match with George when it's really about protecting your dad ... who probably isn't worth protecting anyway." This last phrase she muttered under her breath.

"What's that supposed to mean?"

"He's a criminal, Ari. He helped steal children and sell them as sex slaves. Face the reality. You think you had it hard in the foster system? Imagine what it was like to be raped day after day, hundreds of times a month ... as a child. You can't imagine it, because it's unthinkably, unspeakably repulsive. Your father participated in that, profited from that. Why do you want to save someone so evil anyway?"

It was a good question. One I couldn't answer.

"I better let you get to work," I finally said, grabbing my purse to make a pit stop at the bathroom. Maybe I was pissier than usual because I was PMS-ing. Or maybe I was just pissed because my best friend acted so nonchalantly about my father's fate.

"Not necessary. I'm not going to work today."

"What do you mean?"

She sighed, and I knew it was bad. "I got fired last week."

"Fired? How the hell did you get fired?"

"I dunno. They're sticklers about being there on time, and I was late getting to work too many times. It doesn't matter. It didn't pay well anyway and it was boring. I'll find something else."

"Y'know, eventually there will be no *something else*. You need to grow up and stop being so selfish if you want to be a parent."

The scowl burning through my skin showed me out the door. But I was right, wasn't I?

If Tina couldn't hold down a job for more than a couple months, how was she going to handle raising a child? You couldn't just decide not to feed your kid simply because you didn't feel like it. There was a real chance that finding Giana wouldn't be the best thing for either of them ... but convincing Tina of that wouldn't be easy.

Chapter 9
Ari

My gray-walled cubicle felt stuffy and cramped as I itched to get up and walk around. Even the kitschy black velvet and neon unicorn poster I'd picked up at a yard sale and tacked to my wall couldn't cheer me up. I'd been in a funk ever since the schism between Tina and me widened.

Life was lonely without my best friend. No number of boyfriend kisses or breakfasts in bed or Tristan's handpicked bouquets of wildflowers could mend the ache I felt after my fight with Tina. The best way to make up would be to bring back her daughter ... but I was nowhere close to finding her yet.

I'd spent the afternoon doing busywork, and my legs were growing restless. Even my brain refused to cooperate as it wandered off into worrisome thoughts about Giana, George Battan, my dad. Maybe a coffee would help, since caffeine had an uncanny calming effect on me. Heading to the coffee station—which was essentially a Mr. Coffee coffee pot half filled with day-old brew next to a carton of powdered creamer—I passed Tristan's desk, where he was on the phone. I decided to pop by for a quick hi. Yes, I was that bored that I resorted to pestering my boyfriend at work, despite the warnings about "office romance."

One thing I appreciated most about Tristan was that

he didn't act the part. No tucked-in collared shirt or red power tie. No coffee stains or donut crumbs. He was tattoos and eccentricities, cast from an original mold, with rock star hair and chains clasped to his belt loops. Brooding but funny. Unselfconsciously cool. Even in my worst moods he could draw a laugh out of me. Invigorating like spring water. Just what a thirsty, restless girl like me needed.

Waiting for him to hang up, my eyes wandered over the paperwork scattered across the faux wooden surface of his desk. Notes about the serial killer he was tracking were scrawled on a yellow notepad, gory pictures of crime scenes and evidence fanned out in a collage of torn flesh and tools of death, and I couldn't pull my stare away.

"Find anything interesting?"

I jumped at the question, not realizing Tristan had been watching me. The graphic photos showcased the depths of depravity that lurked in the hidden places and loitered in front of our very homes. Nowhere was safe anymore. Not the workplaces or the schools or the stores or even my own support group. Evil lived everywhere. Even in my own family. I shivered at the thought of a father whose arms held me in a comforting hug then strangled a child to death hours later. Sickening, that's what it was.

"Just browsing."

It was an unspoken rule that I wasn't supposed to nose my way into his cases. Then again, I'd always been a rule-breaker. After I had told him about my little visit to see Battan, I only reinforced this side of me. Luckily Tristan's understanding ran deep, though I wondered how much he'd put up with from me before that well ran dry.

"Browsing crime scene photos? That's not weird at all," Tristan added with a chuckle.

"Shut up."

"How's it going over yonder?"

"Boring. My brain is going numb from all the filing. I figured you could entertain me. Dance for me." I stuck my tongue out.

"You're so mature."

"I know. So, what'cha doing?"

"Wondering what you need."

I winked. "Take one guess. It has to do with you and that apron you look so damn hot in."

He laughed and shook his head. I wanted to kiss the splotches spreading across his neck like raspberry jelly on toast. "You're such a tease."

I lifted one shoulder in a girly pout. "I know. But seriously, I need to pick your brain for a minute."

"Ah, are we gonna exchange the latest serial-killer gossip?"

He knew me so well. "Not this time. It's about Tina—and my dad." I figured maybe he had some advice on how to deal with Tina's little one-woman act, considering he was a cop and all. "I'm sure you saw her media stunt trying to draw attention to the connection between George and Marla ... and then throwing my dad in for good measure."

"I sure did. I thought she didn't want to come forward. Not until she got info on Giana."

"I thought so too. Apparently she changed her mind without telling anyone. I don't know what to do. George won't give me any leads on finding Giana, and the only thing I know is that my father was there—maybe. Can I really trust Tina's memory?"

"She seems pretty certain it was him."

"But a vague memory from three years ago is not enough proof. And I guarantee Dad'll play ignorant if I ask him about it. What other options do I have to find Giana, oh wise one?"

Tristan's lips tightened in a line as he shrugged. "I don't know what to tell you. If we knew the date of birth, we could search public records, but God knows what information was fudged during the paperwork, if there is any. Based on Tina's recounting of her labor, I doubt they ever officially filed for a certificate of live birth with the county. They most likely didn't keep the name Giana, possibly changed the birth date, maybe even crossed international borders. It's been three years—a lot can happen in that amount of time."

"What about Battan? Can you intimidate him into giving details on what he did with Giana?"

"I wish I could, but all we have on Battan is child trafficking charges, which he's trying to get out of. He's got a damn good attorney, and God only knows who he's paid off. Right now I have nothing new to threaten him with. Linking him to Marla's murder was our best bet, but right now it's only hearsay. No evidence, just one girl's word against his."

"So you can't go all Jack Bauer on him and cut off a couple of his fingers or stick a plastic bag over his head to scare the truth out of him?"

"Whoa, I'm a badass, but not nearly as badass as Jack Bauer." He chuckled. "I would love nothing more than to torture him, Ari, but you know I can't. Have you even tried to talk to you father? If you put the heat on your dad, maybe he'll talk. Tell him you know about Marla—see if that gets his lips moving."

I hadn't considered using Marla to get to Giana before. It could actually work if I played it right.

"I guess anything is worth a shot."

I was running out of options fast, but if my dad cared at all about staying out of jail and keeping George as far away as possible, he'd have to start talking. If only I hadn't inherited my stubborn gene from Burt Wilburn, because my dad made a mule look cooperative. But there were ways to get the most mulish of men to talk.

56

Chapter 10

From the Trumpian red tie to the glistening black polish of his dress shoes, Burt Wilburn looked every inch the respectable banker. But I knew Burt's secrets. I knew a demon hid beneath the Ralph Lauren suit, an evil capable of just about anything.

His wife Winnie clung to his arm as they walked to their BMW parked in the driveway. Winnie was clearly the neck in the relationship, turning Burt's head at her every whim. With her upthrust chin she exuded an overweening conceit at having successfully housetrained her pet husband via stingily doling out sex in a reward system, and letting him think he had ideas that were actually his own. Burt wouldn't dare balk at her $200 dye job (that had turned her hair a ghastly shade of red not found in nature) or $80 weekly pedicure, even though he ate brown bag lunches in his office most days. I knew this because I'd been watching.

Perhaps Winnie's love of money was the root of Burt's evil. He'd do anything to please his noose of a wife. But really, in the end she would be the death of him. If not from overworking himself to pay for that dye job and BMW, then from his extracurricular activities with George Battan.

Oddly enough, their home was neither extravagant nor modest—a typical two-story suburban dwelling with modern appeal. Nice yard, cute front porch, a familial hominess yet impressive enough to entertain guests in. With the aid of binoculars, from my angle I could see the gray roots peeking out from Winnie Wilburn's scalp, a stark reminder that a visit to her hairdresser for a touch-up was due any day now. As the hairdresser washed away remnants of her fading youth, did that symbolize the cleansing of sins for dear old Winnie? Was her new look an attempt at hiding who she truly was? Was outward beauty a means to masking her inward ugliness? Perhaps her deception worked on others, but it didn't work on me.

It would take plenty of watching, waiting, lurking in the shadows before I could execute the plan. I was like a soldier reconnoitering an area before a battle—one I was determined to win, if not for me, then for them, the victims.

Burt held Winnie's hand as she settled into the passenger seat, then gallantly kissed her wrinkled cheek—that was a nice touch, Burtie-boy. When it closed, the door made the cottony *whoomp* characteristic of luxury cars; I detested that sound. Then he poured himself into the supple black leather of the driver's seat. The BMW purred to life; Burtie-boy expertly backed it into the street and sped away. I imagined them talking about dinner plans, their favorite dishes, and whether Winnie would have room for her meal if they got an appetizer.

I wouldn't be following them tonight. There was plenty of time for that. Tonight I had other plans. Pulling a black hoodie up to shadow my face and slipping gloves on my hands, I counted the minutes away until I felt confident that the coast was clear. As I was ready to step out of my hiding place, a pair of headlights played across the yard, illuminating the space mere feet from where I hunched down in the shadows. The car slowed in front of the house and rolled to a stop. A woman got out, bounding up to the front door as a drizzle began to fall. Her knock echoed in the evening silence, then again, louder. I watched her scramble through the bushes, then cup her face with both hands as she peered in through a window. The snapping of twigs melted into the soft patter of rain as she crouched her way around the side of the house, toward the backyard, where she disappeared from my view.

Several minutes passed as I watched a light flicker against a window on the upstairs floor. Then a flashlight beam danced across the glass. Who else was intent on unearthing Burt's secrets? I had just enough time to investigate.

Sprinting to her car, I opened the passenger-side door and found the glove compartment where her car registration was tucked into a neat stack of papers.

Ari Wilburn.

Gotcha. And your address too. I hoped it wouldn't be necessary to pay her a visit.

Already things weren't going according to plan, which would require some adjustment. I needed to deliver the letter, preferably in his house so that he knew I was all-powerful, able to easily access any part of his life that I saw fit. But the message couldn't wait. It had to be today, but his unexpected visitor was screwing up everything.

Or perhaps not. Maybe it was better this way. Instead, I headed to the front porch and dropped the envelope on the mat. It'd have to do for now. It didn't matter who found it first—Burt, Winnie, Little Miss Snoopy. In fact, I wanted them all to see it, to know what was coming. Because unlike Scott and Jackson, Burt showed no remorse. I wanted him afraid. I wanted all those who loved him afraid for him. One should know why he's dying, what he's dying for when it happens.

And if Burt thought he could run? Well, I'd be watching and waiting.

As I slipped back into my car, warily looking up and

down the street to ensure no neighbors had spotted me, I wondered just what exactly Ari Wilburn was up to, and how it would impact my own scheme. For her sake, hopefully our paths wouldn't cross again.

Chapter 11
Ari

I didn't know what I was going to say when I arrived at the house I made my earliest memories in. Memories of birthday parties and games of tag. Memories of my sister.

I wondered why my parents never sold the place after years of changed addresses—then suddenly decided to move back in, as if living in the memories was the only way to keep them close. Maybe they felt chained to the house like I did and couldn't let go. Night had already fallen by the time I pulled up the driveway. I needed to prepare my father for what was to come ... though what exactly that was, I couldn't be certain. All I knew was that his name was now publicly attached to Marla Rivers' murder, and the cops would be trailing him for answers ... and there'd be no room for dear old Dad to make a mistake.

I knocked on the front door, freshly painted a new burgundy I hadn't seen before, but no one answered. Knocking again, I heard the dull echo of my fist across the yard. Climbing through the bushes, I crept up to the window that looked into my old living room and peered inside. Darkness. Emptiness. Not a trace of light. No one was home.

The temptation to use this opportunity to dig for

answers pulled at me. I couldn't resist, no matter how illegal it was. Breaking and entering. Big no-no. But then again, these were my parents. What would they do? Turn me in if I got caught? Press charges? Whatever the punishment, it couldn't be worse than when they surrendered me to social services. I was a risk-taker, a gambler. It was what I did best. At only twenty-four, I still packed some hefty girl-balls, and youthful fearlessness was my ticket to misadventure.

A gentle drizzle had started, leaving white pinprick droplets all over my hair. Snaking through the bushes, I headed toward the backyard where I remembered the basement window had never locked properly. As a kid I had discovered it to be a resourceful way of sneaking small animals into the house. Since my mother never ventured into the basement except for twice a year—once to retrieve Christmas decorations, again to return them to storage—I had safely hid my menagerie of caged friends, from injured birds that had flown into the window, to chipmunks that the neighbor's cat had caught and toyed with, until I grew tired of the upkeep and released them back into the suburban wild. As I knelt down to the window, I hoped my parents hadn't thought to replace it.

I tugged up on the lip of the pane. Sure enough, with a little effort it slid upward, stuck halfway up, allowing me ample room to grip the edge to drive it the rest of the way. Once fully open, I squeezed through feet first and dropped to the concrete floor below. The floor was still the pale blue I remembered, the walls a gray cinderblock. The basement had seemed as big as all outdoors when I was little; fallen into disuse, it felt oppressive and claustrophobic. The sharp tang of mold and mildew assaulted my nose as I fumbled for the switch plate. Other than the one window, the basement was completely underground; I wasn't worried about the light arousing suspicion. I found the switch and twin fluorescent fixtures sputtered to life, flooding the basement in brilliant light. There were the animal cages, the store-bought ones and the ones I'd cobbled together from scrap wood and chicken wire, stacked in a lopsided pyramid. Tucked in another corner were the red and green plastic storage bins labeled "Christmas decorations" in Mother's large, precise printing, as if that wasn't obvious from the festive colors. I walked over to them, tracing the words that once upon a time meant so much to me and Carli. Years of dust covered the boxes, and I wondered if Christmas ended with Carli's dying breath for them too. I flicked off the lights, wiped the switch plate for fingerprints, and left the room as I'd found it, a neglected tomb for my memories.

With careful steps I climbed the creaky wooden staircase that always frightened me as a child. Even now my footsteps were hurried as I waited for a hand to reach out between the slats and grab my ankle. The door at the top of the stairs was closed, as I expected. I boldly flung it open, half expecting to come face to face with my father. But instead I opened the door to an eerie silence.

I didn't know what I was looking for, but I'd know when I found it. Dad had always kept an office on the second floor; presumably that hadn't changed over the years. I took the stairs two at a time. Just beyond the landing was the bedroom I shared with Carli. The door was closed but unlocked; I stole inside and a flood of nostalgia overwhelmed me. My parents had preserved the room in all its pink splendor—in tribute more to Carli than me, I cynically assumed. I remembered with fondness all the girly things we'd done, like using each other as guinea pigs for hideous makeovers and poofy hairdos, the late-night bull sessions, crawling into one or the other's bed and holding each other for dear life when thunderstorms raged. Carli never got to grow up, like I had. Survivor's guilt was a bitch. The adult me didn't belong here; I felt like an intruder in my own bedroom, feeding on the memories of strangers. The room was a museum exhibit now, something to be seen but not touched.

I glanced inside my parents' bedroom. A suitcase sat on the bed, open and mostly full. From the doorway I could see my father's khaki pants and collared polo shirts neatly stacked inside. An impromptu trip. What convenient timing.

Further down the hallway my father's office door hung open, and as I walked in I could hear the hum of his computer. With any luck it'd be logged into his account, making my job easier. I slipped inside and sat at his desk. I remembered sitting on Dad's lap as a child at this very desk, spinning us in his chair while he held me tight. I still loved the bastard. Wounds and lies and all.

After scanning his computer files and finding little of interest, I decided to check the desk drawers. Unlocked. My father had always been too trusting. Like the time he'd given me and Carli a family-sized bag of M&Ms unsupervised and made us promise not to eat more than a handful each. As he walked away, we had exchanged looks of incredulity at our father's naiveté as we ate ourselves sick that night. I never did like M&Ms after that.

My father's mania for organization made it easy to flip through the paperwork, once again turning up nothing unusual. Still unsure of what I was looking for, I figured it'd stand out to me when—or if—I found it. As my fingers rifled through paper by paper, a flash of white light crossed the room. In two steps I was at the window, peering through the closed blinds. A pair of headlights skipped across the room, aimed at the house.

Damn. They were home early. I slammed the drawer shut and crouched at the window to see if they had left the car yet, mentally calculating how much time I might have to sneak back into the basement ... or climb out of this very window onto the porch roof below. Years of group homes had prepped me in the art of escape, so this was a piece of cake compared to the Houdini-like breakouts I'd plotted as a teenager. But the car continued to hum, and as I watched, I realized it wasn't their car at all. Someone else was here. But who? Watching me, or watching my parents was the bigger question.

Regardless of who it was, I couldn't be caught here. Crossing around the desk, the floor squeaked under my footsteps. Not the usual creak of achy wood, but a shifting, moving groan. I reached down and pushed it. The floorboard was loose. I couldn't believe it. My father had clearly watched too many spy movies that he would use the old floorboard hideaway rather than a safe. But his lack of ingenuity was my lucky break. Prying my fingernails between the slats, I caught the edge of the plank and pulled at it. It popped off, revealing an empty cavern of space. Aiming the flashlight into the dark cavity, I caught a glimpse of a shape. Something was hidden in its depths. A book. Brown leather and palm-sized.

I picked it up and flipped it open.

Hundreds of names and numbers lined page after page, all in my father's meticulous handwriting. Handwriting I remembered even now from birthday cards of years past—years before they sent me away. It was a banker's script, the thoughtful appreciation of each letter and number as it was crafted by his pen.

As I flipped through it, I realized it was a ledger of some sort. Most likely from his side business with George Battan. The dates went as far back as the 1990s, and I felt my heart splinter that the man I thought I knew during my childhood had been a Grade A phony hiding behind a façade of Kiwanis Club respectability. I had always considered my dad a family man, a dad whose lap I cuddled on, who delivered silly jokes that I'd incorrectly retell to my classmates at school the next day, who made pancakes every Saturday morning for breakfast, who regaled me and Carli with tales of his boyhood memories walking to school in six feet of snow, uphill both ways. As my eyes pored over the countless names and dates and numbers, I had never imagined the extent of his sins to be this great.

I traced the dates to 2002, narrowing it down to April, when Carli had been killed. A large gap of time was missing between November 2001 and April 2002. Apparently he had gone on a hiatus, which I imagined was the reason Carli was targeted. Dad must have tried to bow out, and look what happened. It was a deadly cycle he couldn't escape.

I pulled out my cell phone and took a picture of the pages. A snapshot of the victims, the suffering, the slavery that my own father endorsed, captured in aseptic columns of names, dates, dollar amounts. That was all these lives were worth to him.

I flipped to February 2013, the month and year Giana was born. A specific dollar amount stood out to me. Much higher than the rest. Most of the amounts were costs or income in the hundreds, some low thousands. I assumed those were related to regular payouts to parents who sold their kids off, or incoming payments from selling those same kids' services. But this particular number struck me immediately: $100,000. A tidy sum, too large for any usual service. Not too much to buy a child, though. A baby, in particular. A black-market baby. A red-tape-free baby.

This was the same time Giana was taken from Tina. I read the name next to the 100-grand notation:

P. Baxter

Most likely the name of the person who purchased her.

On the same date was a withdrawal for $3,500 to another name:

E. Peterson

I wondered if there was a connection there. I took another snapshot with my phone, then glanced out the window to see if the car was still there.

Gone. I regretted not getting a license plate number and car make and model, but my heart was drumming too hard and my nerves too frazzled to think straight. I skimmed through the rest of 2013, until I saw a familiar name:

M. Rivers, December 6, 2013

The date Marla Rivers went missing.

A payment had been made in the amount of $2,000 to someone by the name of N. Bledsoe. Probably the man who abducted her, maybe even the same one who murdered her. Flipping ahead to May 2015, my finger trailed down the page as I checked names and dollar amounts. Sure enough, May 23, 2015, another entry for N. Bledsoe in the amount of $10,000. Apparently murder was cheap these days, the life of an innocent child worth less than a Birkin bag. My fury worked its way up from my stomach, warming my neck. Battan had to pay for his crimes.

I wanted to take the ledger with me, see what else I could dig up, but I knew this would be crucial to the police investigation; it had to stay here and be uncovered through the proper channels. But that didn't mean I couldn't use what I was discovering to follow my own leads to finding Giana.

Another picture with my phone, another piece of evidence that I hoped would put George behind bars for life. As for my father, I wasn't sure what this meant for him. No matter what he had done in his life, he was still my father. I didn't want to see him go to jail. But this ledger … it was proof he deserved it. I didn't want to be the one to put him there, though.

I tucked the book back in its hiding spot beneath the floor, replaced the wood exactly as I had found it, and peeked outside one last time. It was all clear. I tiptoed down the stairs, though I knew no one would hear me regardless, and checked the front door locks. Only the doorknob had been locked, not the deadbolt, so I could lock the door behind me without them knowing someone had been inside. It was easier than climbing back out the basement window. Pulling my sleeve down over my hand to hide my fingerprints, I engaged the lock on the knob and exited, hearing the lock click behind me.

Once outside, I noticed the drizzle had slackened to a fine mist. As I stepped toward the driveway, I saw something white on the doormat, obscuring the WELC from the script WELCOME surrounded by yellow sunflowers. An unmarked envelope. With my sleeves again over my hands, I picked it up. It wasn't sealed. I pulled out a folded piece of typical college-ruled paper. A note was messily scribbled in blue ink pen on it, not the studiously precise handwriting as the one sent to me:

I KNOW WHAT YOU HAVE DONE. I KNOW WHAT YOU ARE. YOU CAN'T HIDE YOUR SECRETS. I SEE YOU. I AM COMING FOR YOU. I MUST SOLDIER ON. YOU THINK YOU'VE GOTTEN AWAY WITH IT, BUT I KNOW. I KNOW WHAT LIVES INSIDE OF YOU, BECAUSE IT NOW RESIDES IN ME TOO. THE WRAITH. THE HUNGER FOR MORE. YOU'VE BEEN SWAYED AND SWINDLED BY A DEVIL YOU DIDN'T RECOGNIZE, BUT I'VE GONE WILLINGLY, KNOWING THE EVIL I AM ABOUT TO CARRY OUT. YOU'RE NEXT.

Based on the frenzied scrawl, this was emotional. Personal. Not the cool, collected thoughts of a man behind bars with too much time on his hands, but the ramblings of a psychopath. In the briefest of moments all my fears coalesced into a reality that tasted like bile. Someone knew about my father's involvement. Someone was after him. And I needed to find this someone before they found out what I was up to.

The unanswered questions haunted me yet again. First the letter to me, now one to my father. It was the handiwork of a spineless coward, just like George Battan. But what if I was wrong? What if it was someone else?

I pocketed the letter. I'd pass along the warning so that my dad was prepared, but for now I needed this evidence to point me toward the one behind the threat. Nothing was going to scare me off now. The asshole clearly didn't know who he was messing with.

Chapter 12
Giana

The little girl's black ringlets bounced, brushing against her chubby cheeks as she pumped her legs to go higher, higher, higher into the sky. The swing set vibrated as she swung, the metal legs shifting ever so slightly back and forth under the pull of each ascent. But she didn't notice the subtle lift off the ground, or the squeal of metal. All she noticed were velvety white clouds nudging their way across the blue expanse above—a hippo, a heart, a duck ... and there went a flower.

It was her favorite time of day, the Best Part, when Daddy got home from work and Mommy had fresh warm cookies waiting. Daddy would eat two or three with a cup of coffee while she and Mommy had theirs with milk. Dip, bite, dip, bite. Then drink the chocolately crumbs with the last sip of milk. To a three-year-old, it was perfection. Yesterday was chocolate chip cookies; she wondered what they'd have today. She hoped for peanut butter cookies, but most likely it'd be oatmeal raisin.

After cookies Daddy would probably want to either snuggle up on the sofa and watch a movie together—she always got to pick, and today felt like a *Shrek* kind of day—or play outside while Mommy started dinner. No matter how long the routine played out, she'd never grown bored with it. After all, as Mommy's swollen belly reminded her, it wouldn't be long before things changed. She'd be a big sister soon, which was sure to be a demanding job. But Giana was up for the task. She'd been waiting nine forever-long months for Baby's arrival.

"As big sister," Mommy told her last week, "she's going to look up to you, want to be like you. So it's your job to help protect her and take care of her. Big sisters are the most important people in the world."

"More important than mommies and daddies?"

"Sure. One day you'll want to leave here and find new adventures, and you'll want your little sister to join you. She'll be your best friend someday."

She had nodded understanding, though her smile was uncertain. She couldn't imagine anyone as important to her as Mommy and Daddy.

"I can't wait to meet Baby. I promise I'll take care of her."

"I know you will, sweetie. I can't wait for you to meet her too. Our little miracle baby. Mommy never expected to carry one in her belly."

"Was I in your belly too?"

"Well, you were a special delivery. An angel brought you to us."

Giana's eyes widened with bright curiosity and her mouth opened with a fascinated gasp. "An angel?"

"Yep, you were the gift we'd always prayed for."

Mommy's hug pressed Giana against her hard belly where she felt something poking her.

"Is that Baby?" Giana had asked, placing her palm on Mommy's tummy while Baby rolled around, pushing through Mommy's flowered shirt that always looked so pretty on her. A grape-sized ball thrust out, then vanished, only to appear on the other side of Mommy's stomach. It kind of grossed Giana out, but Mommy seemed to enjoy it.

"She's so excited to come out. Look, she wants to be with you!"

Bending down, Giana had kissed the tiny fist poking through. "I love you too, Baby."

Last week felt like forever ago. When was Baby going to arrive? After two midnight trips to the hospital, still no Baby. The anticipation was exhausting.

She wondered if Baby would swing with her, play tea party with her, eat cookies and watch movies with her. Maybe they could be best friends after all. As the sun warmed her hazelnut-colored skin, Giana felt like today was a perfect picnic day. Maybe when Daddy got home he'd lay out a blanket and they'd eat their cookies on the grass amongst the lilies and pansies Mommy and her had planted in the garden last month. In April. And now it was May. Giana had just mastered memorizing the months of the year and earned a lollipop for her effort. Lollipops sure made learning fun.

In the distance she heard a car door slam shut. From the fenced-in backyard she couldn't see the driveway, but she already knew who it was. Any moment now her mother would call her inside, and the Best Part would begin.

She let the swing slow down its momentum, until she came to a jarring stop as the soles of her sparkly Dora the Explorer tennis shoes skidded against the patch of ground beneath her, stripped bare of grass after months of wear and tear.

The creak of the backdoor opening told her it was time. Then Mommy and Daddy appeared in the doorway, Mommy clutching her belly and Daddy holding a duffel bag. Giana was already halfway across the yard before Daddy spoke, a half-moon smile widening his pink face.

"Giana—it's time for Baby to arrive! Are you ready to go?"

THE DEATH OF LIFE

As she yipped with delight, she knew it was going to be
the Best Part of her life.

Chapter 13
Ari

My fingers hovered over the keyboard. After finishing my shift at the police station, my eyeballs ached and my head drummed an angry beat. I'd been prone to migraines and anxiety ever since I was ten, and I knew a bad one was coming. The slow burn across my temples, the intensifying throb, my lunch churning wickedly ... soon I'd be seeing stars and hiding my eyes behind a sleeping mask while sipping warm ginger ale laced with crushed painkillers.

While waiting for two migraine pills and a coffee to kick in, I had typed into People Finder every possible name and location combination I could think of for P. Baxter in North Carolina, but there were simply too many choices.

Peter Baxter. Patrick Baxter. Philip Baxter. Paul Baxter. Hundreds of Baxters.

So I had narrowed it down to age, selecting only the ones who would be an approximate parenting age. Still, way too many names, way too many variables. I didn't even know if the ones who bought Giana lived in North Carolina. Somewhere George had to have a file on these people, but where? Would my father have copies? Or had they destroyed all traces of a paper trail once the cops got wind of their flesh-peddling enterprise?

A gut feeling told me the Baxters were the ones who had Giana—if that was even her legal name—but it would take a bit more digging to find them. I pulled up the pictures I had taken of pages in the ledger. Another name had gotten my attention, mainly because of the date. The same day the deposit was made by the Baxters. Only this time it was a withdrawal. Perhaps it was made to a lawyer who drafted up fake birth records. Or the person who delivered the baby to the family. There was only one way to find out.

The keys clicked as I punched in E. Peterson, Durham, North Carolina. Only three names popped up on the screen:

Edward Peterson. Eleanor Peterson. Evette Peterson.

I first searched any records on Edward, discovering he was in his early twenties. I jumped over to Facebook to see if he had a profile, and sure enough, he was on social media. His profile said he worked at Duke University in the technology department. Too clean-cut for what I was looking for.

Next I checked out Eleanor Peterson, a single woman in her mid-fifties. As I dug a little deeper, I found her association with several local midwifery groups on Facebook and LinkedIn. A midwife—an interesting fit for the timeline. I slid the puzzle pieces together, creating a picture of how it all connected. George would have hired someone to deliver the baby who was discreet, someone professional but not corporate. Someone he could easily pay to keep quiet.

A midwife.

In particular, Eleanor Peterson.

I jotted down her last known address and checked the time. Not even five o'clock. I could be there before dinnertime if I hurried. With a quick pit stop at the ladies room, I stood in front of the mirror to check my face and hair, which was a blond frizzled mess from the humidity that smothered eastern North Carolina like a wet blanket. My brown irises were islands in angry red seas. I wondered if I was coming down with a cold, or if it was just the sleeplessness catching up with me while I tossed and turned worrying about my father.

Why he deserved my nighttime fixation, I couldn't explain. No one understood it—not Tristan, not Tina, not even me. No matter how angry I was at his decision to cut me out so long ago, someone was after him now. I couldn't let whoever it was get to him.

Rummaging through my faux brown leather hobo bag that fit my entire makeup collection, a variety of feminine hygiene products—which I warned Tristan about in case he ever felt tempted to look through my purse without asking—and my eReader to occupy me during my lunch hour, I pulled out some basic primping necessities. Running a brush through my hair, some eyeliner on my lids, and pressing a hot paper towel to my cheeks, I shook off the exhaustion and tried on my best private investigator imitation:

"Hello, ma'am. I'm Private Investigator Ari Wilburn, and I'd like to speak with you about your relationship with George Battan," I rehearsed, rolling my eyes at how ridiculous I felt. I sounded like a bad actor on a cancelled television series. It was time to take Tristan's advice when it came to interviewing people: be myself.

"You're charming, witty, and down-to-earth. Don't feel the need to force a persona. Just be you. Wonderful, amazing, smart, superstar you," he had reminded me again and again, though I never believed it.

Sometimes I really didn't deserve him.

THE DEATH OF LIFE

Eleanor Peterson lived in a cute two-story gray brick home down a long winding driveway lined with wildflowers, monkey grass, and copses of pine trees green with life. I parked in a graveled pull-off next to a fenced-in garden brimming with herbs and vegetables thriving in moist black soil, a minty scent that reminded me of childhood when I opened the car door. As children we'd had an herb garden comprised of mint, rosemary, basil, and oregano, which Carli and I helped dice for Mom's meals. Beyond the garden was a row of beehive boxes, very active ones that I made sure to stay far away from. After being stung on the eyelid during a neighborhood softball game as a child, bees and I weren't on the best of terms.

A broken stone walkway led to a screened-in porch that was home to an array of clay pots in every shape, size, and color, and at the end of the porch sat a pottery wheel. A bee suit hung on one end of the wall, and a dirty white shelf lined the rest of the way, littered with gardening tools and birdseed. A woman of many interests, apparently.

After I knocked on the screen door, a woman answered, an earthy sort of lady in a flowing pastel skirt and loose flowered blouse that reached her knees. A leather belt cinched the waist, creating a tailored, chic look. Her long brown hair was parted perfectly down the middle. A braided leather headband and granny glasses completed the picture of a gracefully aging flower child.

"Can I help you?" she asked.

"Hello," I began, forcing my best authoritative voice. "My name is Ari Wilburn. I'm looking for Eleanor Peterson—the midwife."

Glancing at my flat stomach, her eyes narrowed. "You don't look pregnant, dear."

"Well, actually, I'm an investigator looking into a man

by the name of George Battan. I believe you know him?"

A frown creased her smooth face. With skin like that at her age, apparently her back-to-nature lifestyle had paid off. Maybe I should consider less pizza and more salads. "I'm confused. Are you with the police?" she asked, her tone blunt.

"No, ma'am. I'm a private investigator. No formal connection to the police. More like an independent contractor." Well, maybe not yet, but I was aspiring to be one. She didn't need to know the difference.

"Then I have nothing to say to you." She stepped back to close the door, but I grabbed the jamb and held it.

"Please, Ms. Peterson." I dropped the act. It wasn't working and I was growing desperate. This was my only lead, slipping through my fingers. "I need your help finding a little girl. A girl I think you helped deliver three years ago."

She stopped and looked at me, empathy in her emerald eyes. She sighed, and I watched the guilt wash over her.

"How did you find me?"

"Through my father, Burt Wilburn."

"You can assure me this conversation will be confidential?"

"I promise. Girls Scout's honor," I vowed, holding up three fingers like I'd seen kids do. I had never been a Girl Scout, but it seemed befitting a promise.

Nodding me inside, she opened the door wide and stepped aside to let me in.

"You seem pretty young to be in law enforcement."

"I get that a lot. I guess I lucked out finding my passion at so young an age."

"And your parents approve of you being in such a ... dangerous field, dealing with criminals and such?"

"You don't look like much of a criminal to me." I

grinned big and received a faint Mona Lisa smile back.

"Looks can be deceiving," she deadpanned.

Eleanor guided me through the house toward a sitting area where several tastefully mismatched chairs dotted the room. There was a funky futon with built-in magazine racks overflowing with seed catalogs and copies of *Mother Earth News*. Colorful teal and orange pillows nestled in the corners of each piece, reminding me of an Indian sari. I was really starting to like this lady.

"Do you like tea? I make a smooth herbal blend from scratch. No pesticides either."

I'd never once given thought to pesticides or hormones or chemicals in my food, but I appreciated the effort. Considering how young Eleanor looked compared to me— thirty years her junior—I figured maybe I should start caring.

"Thank you. I appreciate it."

While she busied herself in the kitchen, I meandered around the living room, noting how uncluttered it was. No family photos. Few knickknacks. Just some artistic pieces purposefully placed on end tables and shelves. Some painted landscapes on the walls. A bookshelf of books on medicine, midwifery, herbal remedies, plant care, and other topical odds and ends. She was definitely more well-read than I was, considering my bookshelf held two college criminal justice textbooks and the rest of the space was dedicated to my shoe collection.

Eleanor flitted in from the kitchen carrying two gorgeous mugs of tea and set them on the "coffee table," a repurposed electrical cable spool she had whitewashed. "Sit!" she commanded, then pattered back to the kitchen.

"Cream and sugar?" she called.

"Yes, please. Thanks."

I sat down in a Queen Anne accent chair whose stuffing threatened to explode from the thin upholstery under my weight. I picked up one of the mugs and examined it. It was roughly blemished, like it had been handmade. The teal was beautifully vibrant.

Eleanor breezed back into the room with a tray holding a cow-shaped creamer and a vintage glass sugar dispenser. She sat down across from me in a peacock chair, fluffing a purple velvet pillow behind her back. The chair suited her; I guessed it was her favorite, and she looked delightfully regal in it.

I helped myself to cream and sugar. "Did you make this?" I asked, tapping the mug.

"No, one of my students did. It was her thank-you gift to me. Pretty, isn't it?"

"Yeah, I'd love to learn how to do this." Though in reality I hadn't the patience for it. Sitting at a pottery wheel for hours on end, molding and reshaping the clay, painting and firing the piece again and again. I'd heard it was a weeks-long project. Too time-consuming for my impulsive nature.

"I teach a class if you're ever interested." "So how can I help you?"

"About three years a girl named Sophia Alvarez was being held captive by a man named George Battan, and she was pregnant. She gave birth to a little girl and that baby was taken from her. I found your name in a ledger for receiving payment for services—Sophia's midwife, I assume. Do you have any idea where that baby was sent?"

A tear glistened in Eleanor's green eyes. "I remember that day. Giana, Sophia called her. I remember your father taking her shortly after she was born. Beautiful little baby. Just perfect. I don't like to think about it, but I had a feeling that day would come back to haunt me."

"Do you know the name of the people who adopted her? I know they paid a lot for her, so I'm assuming it was a black-market adoption."

Sighing, her lips creased into a tight line. "In fact, I do know the family. I had to do several follow-up visits for Giana to make sure she was eating okay and gaining weight properly."

"Wait—did they keep the name Giana?"

"Yes, I mentioned to them that the birth mother had called her Giana, and they loved the name. Wanted to keep it in honor of Sophia."

I groaned. "How noble of them, after illegally purchasing a stolen baby."

"I know it seems horrible what they did—illegally adopting a baby—but they had been through so much. The mother had tried over twenty IVFs—"

"IFVs?"

"In vitro fertilization. They had previous adoption attempts fall through, fostered two kids who ended up getting reunited with their birth parents. All they wanted was a family and things just kept falling apart. They're not bad people; this was their last option for having a baby. And I don't think they were aware that Giana was stolen. I'm sure George didn't disclose that. I hope you understand, they are a nice family."

Did the ends justify the means? Only Tina could answer that.

"I'm sure they're great, but that baby was kidnapped from her birth mother. It's only fair that Giana's mother has a say in what happens. Please, can you tell me where I can find them? I won't mention your name. But Sophia really needs to know what happened to her little girl."

Eleanor glanced away, her eyes glazing over like a muddied sea.

"I don't know ..."

"Please. Put yourself in Sophia's shoes. Imagine if your baby was taken from you, you had no idea if she's alive or dead ... I'm not saying Sophia will do anything beyond seeing for herself how her daughter is doing. Right now that's all I'm asking. Please. You're my only chance of giving Sophia peace after years of torment by George Battan. Doesn't she deserve this one mercy?"

Lifting her mug to her lips, Eleanor sipped contemplatively. Stared into her tea. Picked up a spoon and stirred, then met my pleading eyes.

"Philip and Eve Baxter. They live here in Durham, about twenty minutes away." Then she turned to me, her jaw clenched and stern. "Promise me you'll do what's best for Giana. Sophia was a broken child back then, and she very well might still be that broken girl. You must think of Giana before you go tossing her sweet little life into chaos."

Unfortunately, chaos was a factor I could not control.

Chapter 14
Ari

Oleander Way was an idyllic, Stepford-esque neighborhood of gorgeous mini-mansions, fancy cars, rich husbands, and their tan, slim wives. The seemingly perfect trappings were all superficial, of course; these people had their problems and dark secrets, like any neighborhood. But that didn't stop me from envying—and hating—them a little.

The car idled. I sat in silence opposite the beautiful Tuscan house with stucco exterior, stone accents, and terracotta roof tiles, like a creepy peeping Tom. It was a necessary evil, I kept telling myself, not quite believing it while I stalked an unsuspecting suburban family. The blinds in the Baxter family's living room window were raised, and as darkness settled in for the evening, I could see figures moving inside. I needed a closer look to verify these were the right people. Turning off the engine and sliding out of the car, I gently nudged the door shut, glanced up and down the empty street—noting the immaculate sidewalks and neatly trimmed trees, heck even the road appeared swept—and snuck up to the house. Crouching beneath the windowsill behind the safety of a shoulder-height pyramid-trimmed shrub, I peeked through the cherry wood slats, watching as a family bustled about within.

The mother had set up a stool for a small dark-haired girl to stand on at an island while passing around mixing bowls and spoons and ingredients. Hovering over the child, the mother's arms encircled the girl, entwining her in a swirl of busy limbs as she helped her pour, stir, and mix. The child looked up, a baby-toothed smile of pearly white giggles as the mother smeared a doughy fingertip across her nose, then kissed the smudge off.

Such precious moments I longed for again.

I remembered baking with my own mother, back when she was human and capable of maternal love. Carli and I would fight over who got to lick the spatula, until Mom solved the dilemma by dipping two clean spoons in the batter and handing one to each of us. Simpler times, better times. If only those memories could outweigh all the wrongs committed since.

A movement across the room drew my attention—a tall man with graying brown hair in polo and khakis. An executive type who golfed without fail every weekend, and whose hands never got too dirty, not even when mowing his lush green lawn with his riding lawnmower. He might know his way around an Excel spreadsheet, but replacing a broken fixture was a handyman's job.

In his arms he cradled a baby dressed in pink ruffles. A little girl. So tiny she had to be mere days old. Her frilly-socked feet kicked frantically against Dad's forearm while her arms reached out for his glowing face. Mom approached, hand in hand with her apprentice baker, her chubby cheeks garnished with flour. Holding the baby to his chest, Dad bent over so the little girl could plant a gentle kiss on her wrinkled blond head.

Sisters.

The sweet scene struck a chord in my heart. A deep, resounding, aching song of sibling love.

The little girl tucked into her mother's side bore an

uncanny resemblance to Tina, from the raven hair—even Tina's platinum dye job couldn't keep up with her black roots—to her bronze skin tone, to the cleft in her chin, to the inquisitive brown eyes. A tiny Tina. I noted the mother's dirty blond ponytail and blue eyes, and the father's pale Irish skin, heavily freckled. There was no doubt.

This had to be Tina's little girl. This was Giana.

My eyes stung as I watched them, this perfect little family in their perfect home baking perfect cookies or cake or whatever the hell they were making together. I'm sure it would taste perfect, just like their lives. I'd seen all I needed to see. As I stepped back to leave, the husband glanced up in my direction. Startled, I ducked down out of sight. Had he just seen my black silhouette lurking behind the glass? He might not be so sure. Or he might be certain and start heading out to look for me right now while carrying a baseball bat—or gun.

I crawled on my hands and knees until I was sure I couldn't be seen from the window, then stood up and booked it back to my car. Even after shutting the car door behind me, I couldn't catch my breath. My nervous fingers dropped my keys once, twice, before I finally found the ignition and floored the gas pedal. A glance in the rearview—a long, lean figure stood on the sidewalk across from where I had been parked. Geez, what stealthy detectiving I had done so far, nearly getting myself caught during a stakeout.

The whole way home I worried the dad was tailing me, every few seconds checking my rearview for headlights while taking a circuitous route through various neighborhoods to throw him off. When I felt sure I hadn't been followed, I headed home, feeling ashamed the whole way for getting sloppy and probably scaring the shit out of that poor family. Until today I felt certain this was my calling, the perfect fit for me. Maybe I wasn't cut out for investigative work like I'd thought.

After pulling into my apartment complex's parking lot, I sat in the dark, my cell phone in hand. I could call Tina right now, get it over with, reunite my best friend with her long-lost daughter. I could bring her baby back from the dead. Offer Tina one blessing out of all the pain that she'd been through.

But was it a blessing, really, to take Giana from her home? Or to heap the burden of parenthood on an ill-equipped young adult whose life was in shambles?

As my fingertip hovered over her contact icon in my phone, I couldn't make the call. Tina, an eighteen-year-old jobless nomad with suicidal tendencies. Fit to be a mom? I don't think so. Giana was clearly with the better family—wealthy, adoring, stable, loving. She even had a baby sister to grow up with. Clothing that didn't have that secondhand store warehouse stink. Home-cooked food and a gourmet kitchen with stainless steel appliances to cook those all-organic meals in. Maybe even a housekeeper to clean up after her.

Was it really the right thing to tear this darling child from the only life, the only parents she knew? If what was fair to Tina wasn't fair to Giana, how was I to choose?

There was one person I could talk to. He wasn't the most reliable source of advice, but he would at least understand. At least I hoped he would.

Chapter 15

A target never knows it is a target. At least that's when it's most fun for the one choosing a victim. When the prey knows its predator is coming, well, that simply ruins it all. At least for someone like me. Burt Wilburn, however, was the exception to the rule. I wanted to watch him squirm.

Some men didn't deserve a quick death. Men like Burt, who preyed on the innocent year after year, their own families becoming victims, had earned a special place in hell.

I didn't take pleasure in the kill like others did. Some people got off on it—watching fear contort the face. The eyes drain into lifeless black pools. The blood oozing and seeping. Psychopaths savored it like sinking your teeth into a tender prime rib. Not me. I was no psychopath. The gruesome details did nothing for me. For me it was a job, like a gardener ripping out weeds or an exterminator removing pests. I relished the final outcome—ridding the earth of one more monster.

A monster hunter. That's what I was. One of the good guys.

Fortunately for me, there were plenty of job opportunities. Plenty of villains who needed to be exterminated. Burt Wilburn being one of them.

He hadn't gotten on my radar until after the newspapers linked him to Marla Rivers, a child murder cold case I had remembered reading about years ago, but a little digging told me all I needed to know to seal his fate. Living in the information age had its rewards. Burt's entire life drama spanning the past twenty years all at my greedy fingertips. His youngest daughter, Carli, was killed in a hit-and-run. His oldest, Ari, was mired in the government-run child welfare system. Clearly a horrible father. I knew all about that. Even if that was the worst of his sins, Carli's death was too suspicious to leave him blameless. I had a feeling his own daughter's death was tied back to dear old Dad, and I'd give him a chance to confess right before I killed him.

Routines were everything when planning a kill. It required patience and timing, knowing the predictable behavior patterns of the target. Such as how every night Winnie Wilburn topped off her wine glass before heading upstairs for a bath while Burt lingered behind with his book and coffee, socked feet propped up on the living room sofa. An hour later Burt would check the door locks, tidy up the pillows, then head upstairs to join his wife in the bedroom. I never cared what happened next, as it was the in-between dinner and bedtime minutes that mattered most to me.

From outside their living room window I watched as Winnie, careful not to spill her brimming glass of merlot, teetered up the stairs, her index finger and thumb elegantly holding the stem like she was sipping afternoon tea from her grandmother's china teacup. Up she marched, her ramrod straight back, then legs, and at last slippered feet disappearing from my line of sight as she ascended. One story below, Burt shuffled around the living room collecting things—a newspaper, hardcover book, reading glasses, then lastly his mug of coffee. As Burt sat in a floral upholstered chair, propping his feet on a matching ottoman, I was close enough to see he drank his coffee black—black like the state of his soul. The soul I would today purge.

The great expanse of evening hid me behind a pane of glass, a thin shield between Burt and his bleak future. If I could have, I would have thanked his daughter for her assistance with my plan. Her secret entrance into the house had not gone unnoticed, making my job of breaking in much easier. Dressed in black sweatpants and a black hooded shirt that felt a bit too stifling for this balmy evening, I headed to the backyard, then cracked open the basement window I had watched Ari use.

Funny how people didn't feel the need to double-check their windows and doors in the suburbs. Some people even left their windows wide open to welcome the nighttime breeze ... along with criminals looking for an easy entrance. Didn't they realize nowhere was safe anymore? Didn't they know that children were stolen from their very beds with a simple slice with a pocketknife through a window screen? It was baffling to me.

Though the bigger mystery was Ari Wilburn. I admit I had been surprised when I found out who she was. Their own daughter sneaking into her parents' house doing God-knows-what inside. I couldn't imagine why she was there slinking around the upstairs, but it prompted a deeper dig ... and some questions that only confirmed my suspicions about Burt's character.

Slipping through the window, my feet touched concrete and I worked my way through the darkness toward the stairs. Tiptoeing upward, I turned the doorknob, cracked open the door, and peeked out. Richard Wagner's "Ride of the Valkyries" blared from Burt's top-of-the-line Bose music system. Only the best for the bastard who helped imprison and kill children. I was surprised at his good taste, thinking Burt an uncultured clod. The exhilarating music stirred my blood, providing the perfect soundtrack for my mission.

The interior was as nice as it appeared from my outside vantage point. The scent of a vanilla candle burning wafted to where I stood, back pressed against the wall. From the linens to the matching furniture, everything felt clean and polished, like they were compensating for their sins with mops and dusters, wiping away the dirt from their lives. Maybe I was the only one who saw the stains and the ghosts of Burt's victims.

I rounded the corner that led from the dining room to the living room, watching Burt's eyes study the Lincoln biography he was reading. He looked like a history buff with his glasses perched on his beak-like nose, a student of lives past. I couldn't see the cover from the way the book lay on his lap. Nor did I care. The particulars of Burt's personal library were of no significance; what mattered was stealth and execution. I couldn't risk his wife hearing the noise of our scuffle—I wasn't here for her, she hadn't made it on my list, despite her delinquent mother status—so I needed something to draw him in.

Heading into the kitchen where the granite countertops gleamed and the washed pots and pans sat tidily in the drying rack, I turned the kettle on to boil, then hid in the corner of the hallway that led to the back porch. When the kettle began to whistle, shrieking over Wagner's rousing trombones, Burt's footsteps rumbled down the hallway.

"What the—?" Burt muttered as he turned off the kettle. "And she says I'm the forgetful one. The woman can't remember where her head is half the time," he continued grumbling.

As Burt turned to head back to the living room, I stepped out from the shadows behind him, threw my arms around his chest, one gloved hand holding a dishrag, which I shoved firmly into his mouth to stifle him while the other held a knife to his throat. He shook his head in small panicked gasps, wriggling to break free. But I had the advantage, old man.

Pulling him into me, I whispered into his ear, "This is for Marla Rivers." I raked a shallow inch or two of neck flesh just to make a point, but not enough to do damage. I wanted him to hear the rest of what I had to say, to know why he was chosen, to feel the final thrust that would kill him. The squirming stopped, but the sobs only intensified.

"And this is for all the other girls you've victimized. When you meet the devil at his door today, remember why you're there."

I wanted him to look me in the eyes and know that I saw the fiend inside of him, that Burt Wilburn could no longer hide behind his professionally whitened smile, or his six-figure income. There would always be a reckoning. Circling around him to meet him eye to eye, I held the blade firmly against his throat, but my movements were not swift enough. Beside me his weight shifted, then he dropped suddenly, throwing his arm out to push me away. I leaned forward while he backed away, screaming, and managed to thrust a short jab into his gut. He fell to the floor in a *thump* of blood and whimpers.

"Burt, what's all that racket about?" Winnie called from upstairs.

"Winnie!" he cried out. The Valkyries' ride was building to a crescendo. "Help me!"

As I debated whether to finish the job or run, the floorboards above me creaked as she hurried toward the stairs. It was likely I hit a vital organ; with any luck, he'd probably be dead by nightfall.

"Burt? Turn down the music, won't you? I can't hear what you're saying." Her voice was getting closer. I couldn't wait to ensure Burt's death—not without getting caught or making an innocent woman my next victim.

"See you in hell," I whispered as I fled out the back door, hearing Winnie's screams of terror echo behind me.

92

Chapter 16
Ari

Red lights flashed outside my parents' house when I got there. As my car crawled up the driveway, a gurney passed me in a rush. An oxygen mask covering a face. The thick body of a man. Salt-and-pepper hair. Dad. Two EMTs were wheeling my father into an ambulance as I clumsily stopped the car, jumped out, and ran after them.

"What's happened?" I yelled to anyone who would answer, but no one did. My voice got buried beneath the din of chaos. Uniformed officers taking statements. Nosy neighbors collecting on the sidewalk. CSIs taping off the front door. I tailed one of the EMTs guiding my father, hovering over his motionless body where blood soaked his clothes and bandages stuck to his bare chest. "He's my father. Is he okay?"

"He's been stabbed, ma'am. We're taking him to the hospital," the woman said without looking at me. "Stand aside, please."

I stood there in dumb shock. My father—dead. Gone forever. No last goodbye. I wasn't ready for it. The EMTs hefted the gurney up onto the ambulance platform, then signaled for my mother, who stood a few feet away sobbing into the shoulder of a young cop writing out a police report, her eyes bloodshot, her hair in disarray.

"Mom, what's going on? Was Dad attacked?"

Mom shook her head at me, climbing into the ambulance with the help of the officer.

"I don't know, I don't know, Ari. I found him on the kitchen floor—stabbed."

"What hospital are you going to? I'll meet you there."

Mom looked at me with painful indecision, then cast her eyes somewhere far away.

"Please, Mom. He's my father. I need to be there."

She returned my plea with a nod. "Duke Regional."

I stepped back as the EMTs shut the door behind her, securing her next to my father for what could be his final breaths. The ambulance siren screamed as the vehicle lurched down the road, a heartbreakingly familiar sight. One of the last memories I'd had of home so long ago. The day Carli was taken away after the accident, only to end up dead. And now here was my father in the same horrific circumstances—heading toward an unknown fate caused by some unknown killer out to take him down.

Only this time I wasn't a naïve, helpless child watching it all play out like a movie script. I could do something about it this time; I could rewrite the outcome. I was a woman ready to fight back, ready to fight for my father and my family.

Dad had lost a lot of blood, my mother had told me when we found each other in the emergency room waiting area shortly after Dad arrived in the ambulance, being wheeled through a riptide of scrubs. While the surgeons operated on him, Mom and I sat in stiff silence in the austere waiting room, a stilted camaraderie between us. I hated the pale blue walls, the scuffed white tile, the swish of glass doors opening every few minutes to admit another patient.

And now I hated the dreaded walk to my father's post-operative room in intensive care. A nurse had informed us Dad was out of surgery but was comatose. We were given permission to see him, briefly. Mom went first; I stayed behind to collect my thoughts, promising to come in a few minutes. What I was really doing was stalling. Everything about hospitals made my skin crawl.

Mom sat by his side, holding his limp hand, when I opened the heavy door. It slammed shut behind me, startling her.

"Oh, hi, dear," she said when she turned and realized it was me.

"How's he doing?"

She shook her head sadly. "Still in a coma. They don't know if or when he'll come out of it. All we can do is hope and pray he'll recover."

"And find the bastard who did this," I added.

"Language, please." But she was too exhausted to add any sternness to the words. "I've talked to the police. It was probably a random break-in; it's been happening more often these days. You know your dad—never one to back down from confrontation."

"A break-in? Do you really think that it was some punk trying to steal your flat-screen and jewels?"

Her frail shoulders slumped with weariness. "I don't know what to think, Ari. Who else would want to hurt your father?"

I could name at least one person off the top of my head. I was sure Battan was itching to send a message to my father or to tie up loose ends. With the police questioning the tip connecting them to Marla's murder, this could have been a threat to keep quiet.

Then I remembered the letter. I had forgotten about the note left on my father's front porch. Whoever it was had to be the same one behind the attack—the person outside their house the night I found the ledger. If only I had left the damn letter where I'd found it, my father would have known someone was after him and been prepared. This was my fault. My father barely alive, my distraught mother putting on a brave face, a homicidal maniac still loose ... it was all on me.

The decade-old childhood blame of my sister's fatality hit me like an electric shock. The self-loathing, the torrent of guilt, the endless "if only I had" scenarios that ground into my head like an auger. It all came back, falling on me like a mudslide.

I fell to my knees, sobbing, hands covering my face. When I felt a warmth blanket me, I looked up to find my mother's arm circling my side, a touch I hadn't felt in years but never forgot.

"Hey, baby, it's okay. He'll be alright." She kissed my tears, making me cry even more.

"It's not that, Mom. I think it's my fault Dad got attacked."

"No, you hush now. It's not your fault," she soothed.

"You don't understand." I glanced up at her, afraid to see the disappointment in her face again after these small strides we'd made together today as we clung to each other for hope. But I had to tell the truth, no matter how she viewed me after this. "I did something ..." I paused to sniffle, afraid to tell her. "I'm so sorry." My voice quavered as the apology fell apart.

I never got the words out as she shushed me with her finger against my lips.

"Honey, I don't know what you've done, and I don't care. There's a lot you don't know—nothing that you've ever done wrong. I'm sorry I heaped that on you with Carli, but I'm not going to do it again this time. This happened because of choices your father has made."

I turned away, out of shame or embarrassment, I didn't know. I just felt so vulnerable.

She tilted my chin upward, forcing our eyes to meet. "Hey," she said, "I love you. I love you so much. I'm indescribably sorry for what I've done to you. I can't even put into words how awful I feel, how horrible a mother I was, doing something as unforgiveable as giving you up, but I wasn't well back then. Things were … just so messed up. But we can fix it now. Can you forgive me?"

"Of course," I said without missing a beat, burying my face in her shoulder.

I felt a freedom like flying, soaring carefree amongst the clouds. I didn't have to take the blame for everything wrong in my life anymore. It wasn't my burden to bear. This was on Dad. He'd made himself a target.

Would things have been any better if I stayed out of it and not taken that note? Dad would have gone on the run, making himself a primary suspect in Marla's murder. Either way, he would have had a killer after him, or the cops. Or both. It was a no-win situation for him, but I couldn't shrug off the nagging feeling that I had made his problems worse by hiding that threat from him. And from the cops. Why hadn't I shown it to Tristan? Why was I so friggin' stubborn that I felt I could take on the world?

I knew Tristan would ask these same questions when I told him about the note later today. I had called him from the hospital waiting room, asking him to come, and now I almost regretted it, because I knew he'd give me shit as soon as I told him everything.

I rose from my knees and sat on the other side of my father, closest to the picture window overlooking the parking lot that glowed with the awakening dawn. With my father the divide between us, my mother gazed at me, her age showing in every crease of skin. I hadn't realized just how old my parents had gotten since we'd been apart.

All those years of aging together, lost. I didn't have the luxury of daily or monthly visits. When you spend a lot of time with someone, time's gentle toll on the body—the gradual introduction of wrinkles, gray hairs—goes unnoticed But when you've been separated from a friend or loved one for a long time, your mind becomes hypersensitive to physical changes. The mother I remembered was fresh-faced and big-haired and pink-cheeked and red-lipped. This ragged woman before me only knew how to drag herself from one day to the next.

My father appeared so meek and vulnerable with his hair messily poking every which way. His face looked like a wax impression; try as I might, I couldn't stop my mind from thinking "death mask." I tuned out the disturbing *wooshing* of the ventilator, like a faucet being turned on and off incessantly, as his chest rose and fell with a mechanical rhythm. I couldn't yet come to terms with the possibility that he was involved in a murder. Involved in Battan's financials, sure, like an aspiring Meyer Lansky, dubbed "the Mob's Accountant." But actually killing a child with own hands? No way. Or was there even a difference? He'd taken care of Battan's accounting for years. Didn't that make him just as guilty as Battan? Unless it was under duress ... but if he didn't survive this attempted homicide, I'd never know the truth.

I needed to know.

I needed to know who my dad truly was. A man or a monster.

"Ari," my mother said, her voice quivering, "do you know who did this?"

For some reason I got defensive. "What makes you think I would know?"

She shrugged. "Because you figured out who killed Carli. I never got to thank you for bringing her killer to justice. You gave me, your father, and your sister peace.

Thank you.”

“You’re welcome, I guess. But I didn’t do it for you. I did it for me.”

I didn’t know why I had to add that. I had a chance at a nice moment with my mother and I blew it. I could be such a bitch sometimes, but then again, so could she. That question really poked a nerve. Maybe I couldn’t forgive her for abandoning me, the years of foster care, the loneliness, the self-hatred. Maybe she was right—it was unforgivable.

“I understand. Regardless, it still meant a lot to me that you got justice for your sister.”

“Thanks,” I mumbled. I didn’t know the appropriate response to a thank-you for catching the man who killed your daughter. Maybe one day I would learn it. “And no, I don’t know who did this to Dad. I thought you might.”

“Do you think one of George Battan’s people did this?” She glanced at her hands cupping my father’s, then lifted her chin to face me again. “I guess you’ve pieced things together—your father working with George?”

“I know more than I want to know.”

“So you know about your father’s dealings with that man. Things I begged him not to do, but he was being threatened so he had to. That’s why, Ari. That’s why Carli was killed.”

“I figured as much.”

“And it’s why we sent you away.”

My breath caught. “What do you mean?” Were my ears playing tricks on me? Was I about to get an explanation for over a decade’s worth of questions?

“I was petrified Battan would come after you next. Carli’s murder was a message—a message telling your father to get in line when he said he wanted out. After losing Carli, I feared he’d come after you next. That man”—her voice shook with emotion—“that monster knew no limits, Ari. Women, children, it didn't matter to him. He'd kill anyone without blinking. I sent you away to protect you. I didn't want to—your father and I fought about it constantly—but it was the only way to ensure your safety because I knew he'd never bother to look for you if you were gone."

"Why didn't you ever tell me this before?"

"Because I've been hiding your father's secrets for years. I had to. I couldn't let you find out things that would risk making you Battan's next target. Besides, back then you would never understand it at that age. You were so young. And what would I possibly say? It was better you didn't know. Better for all of us. If you knew and told someone ... I can't bear to think of what would have happened. I couldn't bury another child. The only one I had left."

I was stunned silent. Maybe in the deepest recesses of my heart I had clung to a hope that they gave me up to protect me, but up until now it was just that—wishful thinking. But now ... this confession changed everything. My mother *did* care, always had, even to the point of the greatest sacrifice in giving me up to protect me.

"Do you still blame me for what happened to Carli? I remember how mad you were at me when it happened ... and for years afterward."

"No, honey. I was never mad at you. I was mad at your father. Mad at George Battan. I took it out on you because it was just easier that way. I was heartbroken and scared for your life. Blaming you helped me let you go, in some twisted way. I can't explain it. It's unnatural for a mother to feel this way. It destroyed me. It destroyed you. I don't know what else to say."

As she spoke, the door swung open and Tristan stepped in. Mom rose to her feet as he introduced himself, extending his hand.

"You must be Mrs. Wilburn. I'm Tristan Cox, a detective with the Durham Police." He glanced at me with a question in his eyes, like he was asking for my permission. I smirked. "And Ari's boyfriend."

"Oh, nice to meet you. Oh!" My mother gawked at me while shaking his hand with both of hers. "Are you here for Ari or my husband?"

"Both, actually."

Tristan circled the bed, and I rose to my feet where he waited with open arms. "You okay, babe?" he whispered into my hair as I pressed into his chest.

"Not really," I said honestly. "We don't know if he's going to make it or not. I'm scared."

"I'm gonna figure out who did this to him. I promise."

"What if he comes back?" My mother's voice cut in. "If Burt lives, he'll come back to finish the job, won't he." It was more a statement than a question, for my mother knew all too well how things worked in dirty business.

"Can I ask you a few questions?" Tristan asked. "I know you already covered most of this when the police took your statement, but it'll help me figure out what could have prompted this attack."

Mom nodded. "I'll tell you whatever you need to know. I just want Burt safe."

We all resumed our seats around my father's hospital bed. "As you're aware, Mrs. Wilburn," Tristan began, "Burt's name was mentioned to the press regarding the murder of Marla Rivers. We brought Burt in for questioning and spoke to him, and right now we're still investigating various leads. Can you tell me if Burt had a relationship with a George Battan, whether professional or personal?"

"George was a client of Burt's at East Coast Bank—I'm sure you know Burt managed the Durham branch. Burt had done some, shall we say, private accounting for

George, but when he tried to put a stop to it, George hired that kid to kill my daughter, Carli. I'm sure Ari told you about Carli, right?"

Mom glanced at me, then at Tristan.

"Yes, ma'am, and I'm very sorry for your loss. I'm aware of all the details surrounding that case. It seems Burt did a little more than just accounting though, didn't he?"

"I'm sorry, I don't understand ..." my mother stuttered, her fluster dotting her cheeks.

"Ma'am," Tristan paused, glanced at me, "I already know about your husband's nefarious business transactions with Battan. Clearly it was shady enough that George couldn't hire someone else to take Burt's place—or perhaps Burt knew too much. What I want to know are the details of what Burt knew, specifically pertaining to Marla Rivers."

She sighed. "Look, I don't know the ins and outs of Burt's day-to-day activities, but I do know that he tried to quit working for Battan but the man wouldn't let him. I think Battan hired some goons to try to kill my husband so he couldn't testify against him. I know he's in jail awaiting trial, and I hope he fries." Her voice seethed with hatred.

"But without warning?" Tristan asked. "It seems unlike Battan not to threaten first, because a potential witness suddenly going missing or dead raises an awful lot of suspicion that I think he wants to avoid right now. This isn't *The Godfather*. Even with Carli, your husband was attacked outside of your home as a warning, correct? I'm assuming that was the first time he mentioned wanting out."

"How did you know about that?"

"I know a lot more than you might think. That's why it is important you're honest with me. Don't lie. Don't hide things. For your husband's safety and your own, please, Mrs. Wilburn, tell me everything so I can stop this killer. He's out there, frustrated that he didn't complete the job. He'll strike again. Next time you might not be so lucky."

Tristan's blunt language shocked me a little. Mom took it in stride.

"I don't know what you want from me," she said. "There was no warning. I think it started with the article in the paper tying Burt to Marla's murder. I can't believe they would print his name like that—all because he was brought in for questioning. Isn't that illegal—libel or something?"

"Unfortunately, ma'am, if the media catches wind of something, we can't stop them from printing it. Freedom of the press. But that's not what matters. What matters is that whoever attacked your husband will probably come back. It's highly unlikely that somebody attacked your husband just because the paper mentioned he was brought in for questioning. It didn't incriminate him in any way. My best guess is it's tied to George Battan. But hell will freeze over before we get him to admit anything, so we need any clues we can find to identify the knifer. And until Burt wakes up, we have nothing."

The letter—it was the only clue we had. I needed to tell them about it now, even if it shattered any chance of a long-term relationship with my mother. I couldn't live with lies, not when I had a chance at a clean slate with the only family I had left.

"I have a clue, Tristan."

He and Mom looked questioningly at me.

"A threat letter. I took it off of your front porch, Mom." I sighed. "I was going to tell you about it, get it fingerprinted to see if we could lift a partial."

"Why did you take it?" My mother's eyes blazed with accusation and hurt.

"I don't know. I had stopped by to talk to dad about George Battan, and there it was." I decided to omit the parts where I had broken in and rifled through Dad's illegal ledger. "Handwritten, unmarked, unaddressed. For some reason I needed to open it; I sensed it was something bad. And when I read it, it was a threat."

"And you didn't think to immediately tell us about it?" Mom gasped.

"I was afraid for Dad to read it because I thought he'd try to run, which would only make things worse. After the whole Marla Rivers media circus, I didn't want the cops to question his innocence if he tried to flee. I was trying to protect him, but clearly I screwed up ..."

Her body stiffening, my mother crossed her arms, rose from her chair, and began pacing. "I don't know what to think right now, Ari. You stole something that could have saved your father. He could have protected himself. But worst of all, you put yourself in danger! What else are you hiding?"

"Mom—" I pleaded, but she waved my words away.

"Just stop. Please." She approached me and roughly grabbed my shoulders. "Listen to me, and listen good. I don't judge what you did after everything we've done to you. All the lies. Secrets. Pain. I'm just upset, but not at you. I've already lost too much. Carli, now Burt is in a coma. You're all I have left. What you did could have gotten you killed!"

My mother hugged me then, an embrace I often dreamed about year after miserable year. Her touch was both painful and warming, a confusing mixture of emotions that I couldn't neatly process.

"I need some fresh air. I'll be back, okay?" She released me, kissed me on the cheek, and left, letting the door bang shut.

When Tristan stepped toward me, I knew I was in for

an earful.

"What the hell, Ari? Why am I only just now hearing about this letter?"

"Because I was going to take that letter to Battan to try to force information from him. I have more, Tristan. A lot more."

His eyebrow rose in that cute way it did when something spectacular piqued his interest. "Like what?"

"Well, the reason I was at their house was to interrogate my father about Marla and Giana. You know, kill two birds with one stone. Okay, bad choice of words. They weren't home so I decided to break in and snoop around. And before you yell at me, I found something. A ledger."

"Please tell me you didn't take it, because it would be inadmissible in court."

"I know, I know. It has to be legally obtained. I'm not a friggin' idiot. I only glanced through it then returned it where I found it."

"Did you touch it?"

"Don't worry, I was careful not to leave fingerprints. I took some pictures of the transactions around Marla's death then put it back." I didn't bother to mention the dates of Giana's birth. That was between Tina and me, and I needed to keep it that way for now. I still didn't know how I was going to handle that drama.

"It's tucked safe and sound where I found it for the Durham Police to stumble upon. But it shows large sums withdrawn right before Marla's murder—and partial names. Presumably Battan paid the killer—and fairly well."

"How does this link to Burt's attacker? You think it's Battan?" Tristan sounded almost excited.

"Actually, no. So, while I was inside I saw a car waiting out front. By the time I got outside the car was gone, but the letter was left behind. I don't know if he wanted me to find it or not, but I did. And it didn't sound like a threat to keep quiet. It sounded more *I Know What You Did Last Summer*. Like this person knew my dad's secrets and was gonna make him pay."

"Shit." Tristan propped his hands on his hips and walked to the window, stood, and gazed out.

"Shit what?"

"This sounds like the MO of that serial killer I'm tracking. This guy is some sort of vigilante on a warped personal crusade, but I'm not sure why these men are targeted. There's no apparent connection. And they're all clean. Like Scott Guffrey. Stabbed to death in his living room. No record. Liked by everyone, even his ex."

"Was there a note or anything that we could compare the handwriting to?" I asked.

"Not that we could find. Then we have Jackson Jones, also stabbed to death in front of his house in his car. No note, but he had just returned home from your suicide support group when he got murdered. You said you vaguely remembered him—right before I showed up in April."

I remembered that day well, when I first saw Tristan and probably said something incoherent and dumb, though I couldn't remember what. I had been smitten ever since.

I shrugged. "The group's anonymous. If he's the guy I think it was, I think he used the name Joe, not Jackson. What'd he look like again?"

"Nerdy kind of guy with glasses, brown hair, brown eyes. His wife said he was soft-spoken, kind of shy around crowds. Sound like anyone you might remember?"

Tristan described half a dozen men who had attended, and over time if they didn't return, the faces all began to blur together.

"Ah, so that's why you showed up at the meetings—hoping to find the killer in the group?"

"That was the original reason. But it actually helped me work through some depression issues I had." Tristan avoided my gaze as he spoke.

"Depressed—you?"

Tristan the jokester, the adventure-seeker, the never-a-dull-moment kinda guy. I found it hard to imagine someone so confident and outgoing ever feeling lonely or sad.

"Sometimes life gets rough. It's not all unicorns and rainbows in my world, you know."

Boy, did I know it. I had been the master of facades.

"What makes you think these guys were targeted and not just random attacks?" I asked.

"Too organized. Too clean. The killer knew his victims. He knew the layout of their homes. Knew their schedules and routines. Scott had a son, and the killer knew when his son wouldn't be home. Jackson's wife was at work when he was murdered. With Burt, he had watched your parents long enough to know that Winnie would be upstairs at a certain time, like clockwork. It seems to fit this killer's methods. Which leads me to believe he knows something about Scott and Jackson that would warrant their execution—because ultimately that seems to be what this case is all about: a vigilante who's appointed himself judge, jury, and executioner."

"Any ideas what they might have done?"

"Scott had been questioned in the disappearance of his fiancé's daughter's disappearance almost two years ago. But police ruled him out as a suspect. A body was never recovered, and all evidence pointed to a break-in. Plus, where it happened is a popular place for sex traffickers to pick up children," he explained. "Very rural, lots of unsupervised kids running around. We couldn't pin anything on Scott so we let him walk. Maybe the killer knew something about it that we don't ..."

Sadly, it wouldn't be the first time a stepfather had killed his stepchild.

"What about Jackson Jones?"

"Clean as a whistle. And no connections to Scott. Works in social services. But why was he in your suicide support group? Was it from guilt over something? Something that the killer knew about? That one baffles me."

"Or maybe the killer is just assuming things," I wondered aloud. "Since my dad's name was printed in the paper alongside George Battan's in connection to Marla's murder, maybe that's why the killer targeted him. But we don't even know that my father was a part of that. I don't think he is. If this same killer attacked my dad, then he's not doing his due diligence. I want to help you find the son of a bitch."

Whoever it was that had assaulted my father, putting him in a coma. It was personal now and I had a vendetta to wage.

"Hell no, Ari. We're dealing with a man who has killed two men and nearly killed your father. I'm not letting you anywhere near this case."

"What makes you think it's a man?"

"Because these men were overpowered. Even though your father's older, he's no wimp. Plus the angle of the blade and the locations of the wounds show the person was at least five-foot-nine. That's getting tall for a woman."

"Not really *that* tall."

"But taller than average."

"So it's possible it's a tall-ish woman," I pushed.

"Ari, please drop it. I'm not saying you're not intelligent enough to figure it out, because I know you are. But in law enforcement you need support—people looking out for your back, covering for you in dangerous situations. You don't have that insurance when you're going solo. For now please stick to filing and your coursework. You'll get to do the investigative stuff soon enough, but you have a lot to learn first."

"Can I at least talk through the case notes and evidence with you—you know, all that learning shit you want me to do?"

"As for the *learning shit,* yes, I'd love to."

Chapter 17

Two years ago ...

Although Kathryn Brannigan was only five years old, she was an old soul—independent, unusually inquisitive, more sensitive and mature than her peers; in a word: *different.* As she looked up at Scott Guffrey, the tears in her eyes brought the green and yellow flecks to life, like little goldfish swimming in shallow pools. "Such deep eyes," her mother Helen often said of her. "Like beacons of hope for a better future."

Helen dropped three generic brand chocolate chip cookies on a plate and filled a glass half full with milk. The milk jug was almost empty and they were still a week away from payday. They'd have to ration it until then. *Maybe half a glass is too much,* she thought as she poured some from the glass back into the jug.

Setting the plate down on the coffee table stained with crusts of food that, left to harden, were now barnacled into the surface, Kat muttered a "thank you, Mommy" between bites. A simple treat to wipe away the tears. It never failed.

The living room floor slanted slightly toward the far wall, which Kat appreciated as she'd release balls and watch them race along the dirty carpet, but for Helen Brannigan, it was just one more reminder that her trailer was falling apart. Along with her life.

Things should have been looking up. She was engaged to a wonderful, hardworking man, Scott Guffrey—a solid two steps above her ex, Kat's father, Cody. Together Scott and Helen created a plan for the perfect future for their blended family. Once they got married they'd get rid of the trailer and buy an affordable four-bedroom house and the new, better life that came with it. Kat and her little sister Tempest would each get their own rooms; so would Mikey, Scott's son. With Kat now in kindergarten and Tempest starting school the following year, the paycheck-sucking daycare costs would end and they'd finally have extra cash—something Helen hadn't enjoyed the luxury of, well, ever. At least not since having kids.

Trailer park life was a sadistic cycle. The meth addictions that held so many captive. The home burglaries that funded the addictions. The crummy, congested living quarters. The absence of a safe yard for the kids to play in. The scarcity of decent jobs. The underfunded schools. In Kat's case, they were lucky enough to live on the outskirts of a wealthy school district. At least they had thought themselves lucky. Boy, were they wrong. Mixing snooty, entitled kids with proud, needy kids with chips on their shoulders was a recipe for disaster. Sometimes it was all-out class warfare. The poor kids that didn't stick up for themselves got pushed around. Kat was a scrapper and never backed down from a fight.

Bullying—the new epidemic. A form of psychological torture that made military interrogation techniques look childish. Back in Helen's day bullying took place on the playground where you could fight it out or walk away. A snide remark or two, usually intercepted by a teacher. Nowadays it was a barrage of premeditated attacks, not just in school, but in the very bedrooms of kids active on social media. There was no escape from the insults, the filthy rumors, the false accusations when they followed you home on your Facebook or Instagram or Twitter accounts. Luckily Kat didn't have these luxuries, but

Helen knew the reality: the bullying would only get worse, grow bigger, like a hurricane gathering speed and power as it headed for shore.

Things had to change before then. They needed out of this town, out of this downtrodden trailer park, out of this helpless school with its ineffective policies and hapless teachers who concerned themselves more with appeasing parents than stopping a pint-sized terrorist from sending Kat home in tears day after day.

Enough was enough.

All Helen wanted was for her daughter to fit in. Be happy. Such a simple request, really.

It'd all change soon. Maybe they could finally get Kat out of this school and into one without Sophie, the entitled brat whose parents ingrained in her that she was a princess and poor people were meant to serve her every whim. The moment Kat refused she became the target of Sophie's endless torment. Kids could be so cruel.

Hence today's sobs and sniffles and hugs and cookies … again.

As Scott and Kat exchanged whispers on the sofa and Tempest napped in the girls' shared bedroom, Mikey walked in from the back porch, the spitting image, Helen imagined, of his father when Scott was three, going on four. He was a devil-may-care boy's boy in the Tom Sawyer mold, with mud on his face, caked in his hair, grass stains on his clothes. There was no escaping bath time tonight.

"You digging for worms again?" Helen asked him.

"Yup, found four!" He held out three chubby fingers. Sliding onto the empty cushion on the other side of Scott, he said, "Hey, Daddy. Whatcha doin'?"

"Hey, bud. Just hanging out with my best girl," Scott answered, squeezing Kat into a burst of giggles.

"Can I have a cookie too?" Mikey asked, pointing at the

remnants on Kat's plate.

Shoot. Helen had given the last ones to Kat, which she now regretted because of the growing rivalry between the two kids. "Sorry, Mikey. Those were the last ones, but I promise to get you whatever kind you like when I go to the grocery store, okay?"

Huffing an okay, he crossed his arms and pulled his knees up to his chest while his father continued to dote on Kat.

"It's okay, sweetie," Scott said as he pulled her closer to him. "You want me to take care of Sophie for you? I'll show her who's boss." He flexed his biceps and Kat laughed as crumbs spurted like a sprinkler from her mouth.

"How 'bout you give it a squeeze?"

Kat reached up and poked at his arm muscle.

"Hey, Daddy, look at my muscles." Mikey excitedly held out his arm, pulling his sleeve up above his thin, little-boy-sized bicep.

"Those aren't muscles," Kat jeered.

"No, these are muscles, Mikey." While Mikey frowned, glaring jealously at his soon-to-be-sister, Scott's arms did a brawny dance. "These guns will scare off the meanest of girls."

"That's about all they'll scare off," Helen teased from the kitchen as she loaded the dishwasher.

"Hey, this is an A and B conversation, so C your way out of it."

Helen groaned. Scott, a boy stuck in a man's body. "I haven't heard that since I was Kat's age."

"It's a classic."

Scott flashed her that charming grin he used to win her heart months ago when they first met. Scott had walked into the bar where she bartended, showing off with his buddies from work as he slid up to the bar top and ordered a round of beers for everyone. She couldn't help but roll her eyes at his blatant attempt to impress her, which she secretly appreciated. It'd been too long since a man showed her any attention. In her twenties it was easy to get a slap on the butt or a whistle; now in her late thirties with two kids and a body that showed it, she felt like she'd been mummified.

Helen had reached the stage where she could take or leave male companionship. She was no slut, having only been with two men in her life—her husband Cody and now her fiancé Scott—and she had always been self-confident in her looks, even during the many weight fluctuations that came with a slowing metabolism. But when your tips are based on attractiveness and flirting, well, it's a lot better to get ogled and pay your rent than be ignored and barely scrape by.

Luckily Scott took that variable out of the equation when he sauntered into her life wearing cowboy boots, tight-fitting Wranglers, and a cowboy hat that hung just low enough to shade his eyes and add a dose of mystery to the face beneath the brim. As he placed his hat on the sticky bar counter, she noticed him right away—incredible blue eyes, curly blond hair that instantly made her think of Matthew McConaughey, and a lithe body that made her want to unbutton that blue work shirt he wore with his name embroidered on a Drew's Plumbing patch: Scott Guffrey.

A nice, solid, reliable name, as far as names went.

The $100 tip was nice, sure, but what really got Helen's motor running was Scott's attentiveness. He barely took his eyes off of her and lavished her with little compliments that sounded sincere and unrehearsed, nothing like the tired, often crude lines she parried on a nightly basis from drunken Lotharios. For the first time in years Helen felt special and beautiful. She'd never bought into the whole cornball "swept off your feet" thing, but now that it was happening to her, she didn't resist. They'd embarked upon a whirlwind romance and never looked back.

The best part was that the girls loved him too. Their stamp of approval was make-it-or-break-it for any potential boyfriend, and since Scott had a son of his own, he knew kids. He knew how to play with them, hug them, tuck them in at night, sing to them, even discipline them, which he never did, of course. He was all play, which was just fine with Helen. As she watched Scott ease Kat's woes with a kiss on her sweet head, Helen felt like all was right with the world.

"I don't want to go back there," Kat whined into Scott's arm as she leaned into him. "Why can't I stay home with you? You could be my teacher!"

"Don't you worry, honey," he whispered secretively in her ear. "We'll be out of here very soon. You'll never have to deal with that mean girl again."

In his little unnoticed corner, Mikey wished he'd never have to deal with Kat again.

Chapter 18
Ari

It's been too long, honey, too long."

"I know, Mrs. E. I've missed you over the years."

Mrs. E, as I had called her since I was five years old and first allowed to talk to the neighbors, was short for Mrs. Eidenschink. Not a single person referred to her by that mouthful. It was common knowledge that she preferred plain old *Mrs. E*; the friendly moniker had stuck with everyone up and down the street. We had been across-the-street neighbors until I was sent away, and I hadn't seen her since. On particularly boring nights at the group homes I'd reminisce about sneaking across the street to accept baked treats from her while she gardened. By gardening I mean placing hundreds of gnomes, birdhouses, angels, and a mishmash of tacky lawn ornaments all over her yard. And I mean not a patch of grass was left untainted by the eyesores as Carli and I would make a game of navigating through them like Indiana Jones to reach our trophy: that day's freshly baked goodies. While most people found Mrs. E odd and kept their distance, I appreciated the eccentricities that made humanity, in its infinite variety, so colorful.

"How have you been?" I asked, sitting at a kitchen table surrounded by yellowed newspapers on one side and a lampshade on the other.

THE DEATH OF LIFE

When I'd decided to visit Mrs. E and she'd invited me inside, I was unprepared for the assault on my senses. First there was the pungent ammonia smell of cat pee, which my eyes and nose followed to an overflowing litter box in the foyer. A scruffy marmalade cat with a corkscrew tail had just finished doing its business (loudly and stinkily) and eyed me with cold feline indifference. I remembered the ranch-style house as being clean and cozy, with a lived-in vibe: an inviting place to visit. Now the foyer was the only hospitable spot in the house—a clearing in the impenetrable jungle of what I instantly perceived as Mrs. E's late-life hoarding disorder. Piles of boxes, knickknacks, books, old magazines, and motley of junk took up every wall, every corner, practically every inch of space. Out of pure necessity Mrs. E had blazed a narrow path that wended its way throughout the detritus littering the once spacious house. It was this path we followed to the kitchen, where Mrs. E cleared out a small space for me to set down my coffee mug, and then joined me at the table. It was a wonder she could find a clean dish amid the phone books and useless garbage stacked along her counters—if the mug was indeed clean to begin with. It took sheer force of will to take a sip—purely out of politeness—as I considered her offer.

"Been okay. Arthritis acting up as usual," she replied.

"Keeping the neighborhood kids in check?"

Mrs. E chuckled, her wide lips painted in red lipstick. "Oh, Ari, I can't keep up with them these days. I feel slap wore out most of the time. What about you—how are you, dear? Got a husband yet?"

The ever-asked question of a barely grown woman in her early twenties. I imagined the questions persisted with age. *Married yet? Kids yet? Mortgage yet?*

"I'm only twenty-four; got plenty of time."

"Honey, by age twenty-four I had been married six

years!"

"Don't worry, Mrs. E. I'm not doomed for spinsterhood. I'm actually dating someone special."

Her black penciled eyebrows rose, only accentuating how crooked they had been drawn on as her hands trembled. The wrinkles didn't help matters. At least the brows matched half of Mrs. E's black dye job—the half that hadn't grown out in a shock of white roots.

"Bring him on by sometime and I'll whip up some *golabki*." I remembered Mrs. E bringing this Polish dish over shortly after Carli's funeral. The word had reminded my ten-year-old self of *glob*, which was exactly what it had looked like to me then and still did—cabbage, spicy meat, and rice mixed together in an edible, well, glob.

"Sounds wonderful. I'd love to take you up on that. I know he'd instantly like you."

"You're such a doll," she beamed. It'd probably been ages since she'd spent quality time with someone who wasn't her cat. "Tell me what's new with you. I'm low on gossip since Ethel died last year."

"Well, I'm a private investigator now." So I stretched the truth like a long string of gum, but Mrs. E wouldn't care about the particulars.

"Ooh, fascinating! Like Dick Tracy?"

"Uh, sort of, yeah. Which is why I'm here, actually."

"Let me guess." She placed a skeletal finger against her gaunt cheek and gazed upward in thought. Mrs. E always had a flair for the dramatic. "It's about your father, am I right? You know I always keep an eye on things 'round here."

"I knew you'd come through for me," I affirmed with a wink. "I'm sure the police have talked to you too, but I was hoping maybe I could find out if there's something they missed."

"I'll tell you what I told the nice officer who stopped by.

It was around nine o'clock when I was settling down for the night. Lucy—that's my cat—started meowing at me to go out, and just as I let her out I saw a person in sunglasses walking at a brisk pace down the street. I thought it odd—sunglasses after dark. Who does that? But that's all I saw, unfortunately."

"Do you know anything about what the person looked like? Could you tell if it was a man or a woman? Race? Any facial features or distinguishing marks? A limp? Anything at all?"

"Let's see." She tapped her sharp chinbone. "He was wearing a black hoodie, so I couldn't get a look at his face. Whole body covered in black."

"You think it was a *he?*"

"What other kind of criminal is there? It's always a man."

I didn't want to correct her that plenty of women led criminal lives too, so I let her go on.

"I'm 95 percent sure it was a white person. It was dark, so it was hard to tell."

"What about his body type? Thin, thick?"

"Skinny, I'm pretty sure. It wasn't a bulky kind of body, and his clothes hung on him loose-like. Very slender. Not real tall, either, I don't think. Though, I could be wrong. My memory isn't what it used to be. I wish I could be more help."

I rested my hand on her knuckles that nearly jutted through skin as thin as tissue paper. "This is definitely helpful. I'll keep you posted. And we'll figure out a time to do dinner together, okay?"

She smiled, revealing her coffee-stained dentures.

"Thank you, Ari. Don't be a stranger, y'hear?"

With a gentle hug—I feared breaking her brittle bones—I left knowing that this narrowed down the suspect list to pretty much ... anyone. Possibly male or female. And maybe white. Slim. Not too tall.

Great.

I slipped into my car and sat in thought. I was convinced that my father's attacker was the same person who killed Scott Guffrey and Jackson Jones. As Tristan had pointed out, same MO, same knife wound, all connected to my suicide support group in some way. Something trusting about this killer let these victims invite him or her into their homes.

My mother hadn't heard a peep while my father had gotten stabbed. If the killer was a man who barged his way in, wouldn't my father have cried out for help? A woman could have manipulated her way inside. But then she'd have to look pretty suspicious wearing a black hoodie when she showed up. After all his dealings with Battan, my father knew better than to invite strangers into his home.

Something about these three victims was connected, but what? I had to find out what linked them to this killer if I was going to stop him from finishing the job with my father. I rummaged through the center console for the pen and tablet I kept in the car for when inspiration struck and began jotting down the things I knew:

All three victims were men.
All three attacked in their homes or in front of home.
Suicide support group pamphlet found at Scott's house—depressed, contemplating suicide?
Jackson attended group meeting—why?
Killer linked to suicide support group?
Two of the victims were connected to missing girls—Scott and Burt.
Scott's gf's daughter, Kat, had gone missing. Did he have something to do with it—cause of depression?
Burt was connected to Battan, who was behind Marla's

murder.

Jackson—who was he? What was he hiding?

Find out Jackson's secret—the key to how it's all connected?

Chapter 19
Ari

My first step to figuring out how the victims were connected—if there even was a logical connection, given serial killers' typically twisted reasoning—required digging into each victim's past. With no clear work or recreational similarities among all three, it had to be something obscure that tied them together in the killer's mind. Their secrets, their veiled lives, their transgressions—that's what I was after.

It wasn't hard to unearth everything about Scott Guffrey when I Googled his name and a dozen news reports popped up online about his relation to Kathryn Brannigan, daughter of Helen Brannigan, who was his fiancée at the time. Then shortly after Kat's disappearance Helen became his ex. The question was why. I was pretty sure it had to do with Kat's presumed death, but there had to be more to the story. There always was.

After a quick search for Helen's last known address, I headed out. As soon as I pulled up to the ramshackle trailer, I could feel the strife, the ache, the sorrow that plagued this place. Row after row of godforsaken dwellings covered in mildew, walls chewed alive by rust, roofs sagging and ready for the meager weight of a falling leaf to send them tumbling down. The park was surrounded by kudzu monsters—trees transformed into fascinating grotesqueries by the bane of the South, an invasive vine introduced to check erosion, but instead gobbled up and strangled everything in its path. The kudzu grew up the sides of some of the trailers too, sticking its insidious fingers into seams and cracks. In urban slums human neglect was housing's worst enemy. Here, there was another, more chilling wrinkle: Mother Nature slowly but inexorably reclaiming what was Hers.

I waded through knee-high weeds to the front door, running a gauntlet of broken toys and stuffed animals, their googly eyes staring disconcertingly up at me from their ruined bodies. The screen door dangled dejectedly from its sprung hinges, and the roof held at least a decade's worth of debris. The whole trailer slumped like it was too weary to hold itself up anymore, making me wonder just how much longer it had before it collapsed into a depressed heap. A set of termite-chewed wooden steps led to the front door, crumbling under my weight. I wondered if the trailer represented the state of Helen's soul after losing her daughter.

I held the cattywampus screen door open with my knee and knocked on the alligatored, cow-patty-brown main door, a dull thud that I doubted anyone could hear over the television blaring inside. The walls were so thin I could overhear people talking inside, so I knocked again, harder. This time a woman inside screamed, "Turn that TV down!" her voice growing louder as she neared the door. A moment later the background noise died and the doorknob rattled.

The first thing I noticed was the height of the woman who answered. Easily five-foot-ten. And skinny. Almost-never-eats skinny. Her black hair was cut into a chin-length bob that had probably looked chic at one point but had grown out to lay flat and lifeless against her sharp jawline.

"Hi, I'm Ari Wilburn. I'm looking for Helen Brannigan?" She shifted to prop her hand on one jutting hip.

"That's me. Whatd'ya here for?"

"I'm a private investigator, and I'm looking into your daughter's disappearance about two years ago."

"Lookin' into it how? The police haven't contacted me about anything."

She was clearly guarded, tense, unwilling. I needed to break down the wall that divided us if I was going to get anything worthwhile from this trip.

"Can I level with you? My father was recently attacked—almost killed—and I think it might be connected to your daughter's disappearance. I believe that the person who tried to kill my dad knows what happened to Kathryn."

"Kat," she corrected. "We call her Kat."

Present tense *call*. She clung to a hope that Kat was still alive.

She stepped aside, holding the door open for me. "You wanna come inside?"

"Yes, thank you. I really appreciate this."

I followed her into what she probably called the living room, but what anyone else would call a personal injury lawsuit waiting to happen. Within five steps forward, a foot-sized hole peeked through the floor to a patch of earth underneath.

"Sorry, watch your step. We had a roof leak and the floor got so wet it broke through." A defeated look clouded her face. "Been meaning to fix that."

Despite the trailer's ramshackle state, the room was neatly organized. Toys in a wicker basket in one corner, books stacked tidily on a small bookshelf. On a clean sofa a little girl watched a DVD of the Disney animated feature *Frozen* while eating Cheetos. Crumbs fell in her lap and her fat little fingers turned a brighter shade of orange with every bite.

"Make yourself comfy. Want some coffee?"

"Sure, that sounds great." While I hated to accept an offering from this penniless family, I needed a kick of caffeine after this morning's early rise. I hated mornings, hitting the snooze button on my alarm at least five times before I could force myself out of bed. Tristan was convinced I was a vampire.

"Hi," I greeted the little girl while Helen stepped into the kitchen. And I mean one step. The house was smaller than it looked from the outside. "I'm Ari."

The girl glanced up at me and grinned. "I'm Tempest. I'm six years old. Have you ever watched this movie? I've watched it at least a bajillion times." Her cheeks were full of food as she chattered, and I felt a light spatter on my cheek as I sat next to her. The TV was a big, boxy CRT model, at least twenty years old; the remains of a yellow Goodwill sticker clung to the chassis. I recognized the Craig DVD player as a cheap model sold at Dollar General, a discounter I wasn't too proud to admit I'd shopped at with some frequency. *Frozen* was nearing the part where Anna met Olaf. I would never admit it to Tristan, but I had watched it so much that I memorized the entire movie and could sing every song ... and I often did while in the car, the shower, or pretty much anywhere alone.

"Oh yeah. I love this one. Who's your favorite character?"

Her cheeks flushed pink. "Elsa. I like her hair."

"Me too! Though Olaf makes me laugh, so I guess I like him a lot too."

Helen sat down next to me, handing me a cup of coffee. "Sorry about that." She nodded toward Tempest. "She's my little chatterbox."

"No, don't be sorry. I love kids."

She leaned in to me and said conspiratorially, "Well,

don't let her catch wind of that or else you'll be stuck here all day," adding normally, "So whatd'ya wanna know?"

I didn't know where to begin. I had looked up the case records at work the day before, but there wasn't much to go on. No body found. No witnesses. Only a ripped screen in Kat's bedroom window and several sets of boot prints outside the house, which could have been from anyone. Scott had been living with Helen at the time, and the ex-husband, Cody, had custody every other weekend. According to the case file, Cody had been a primary suspect in her disappearance based on his record—domestic assault. Several times against Helen, but he never touched the children. Apparently the man had a bad temper, but even Helen admitted he had nothing but hugs and kisses for his little girls, and he'd kill anyone who laid a hand on them. Just because he couldn't keep his hotheadedness in check with his wife didn't necessarily mean he killed his daughter. And without a body, no arrest could be made.

And that's when the trail—and case—went cold.

"From what I understand, Kat was taken from her bedroom while she was sleeping. Did you ever have a hunch on who would have abducted her?"

"At first I thought it was Cody—my ex—trying to make a point. He had never been thrilled with the divorce, and hated the custody arrangement. But after he beat the crap out of me one night I decided it was the last time and I feared for the kids' safety with him having a temper like that. Lord, if he ever beat the kids like he did me ..." She shook her head and closed her eyes as if pushing the images away. "I can't bear to think about it."

I wanted to hear her personal corroboration of the case file. "Did he ever hurt the kids?"

"No, never. The man adored them. Even basic discipline was always left up to me to handle. Wouldn't spank them, barely even raised his voice to them. They were his angels, as far as he was concerned. Spoiled them rotten, too. Thought it was cute how they favored him over me. But still ... I always had reservations about them being alone with him after how he treated me. You never can be sure, y'know?"

"I'm glad you had the courage to walk away. That must have been hard."

"Going from two incomes down to one was the hardest part. I knew getting child support payments would be like pulling teeth." Glancing over at Tempest, Helen placed her hands over the child's ears. "But getting away from that wife-beating prick was the best thing I ever did."

Pushing her mother's hands off her head, Tempest whined and returned to her world of ice and catchy melodies. I saw that she was oblivious to the adults' discussion. Still, I instinctively kept my voice low, and Helen followed my lead.

"Any idea why he beat you?"

"Well, mostly 'cause of the guys that hit on me where I work. I bartend. Back in my prime I had it going on. Cody'd get all jealous when I'd come home with good tips 'cause he thought I did something extra to earn them." She air-quoted the word "extra" and rolled her eyes. "Thought I flirted too much. Duh! You gotta flirt if you want good tips. That's the whole friggin' point—excuse my French. But I never did nothin' more than flirt. Cody was convinced otherwise. Then he'd beat me. So I divorced his sorry ass."

I wondered if the family drama swirling around them could have set Cody off.

"Do you think he took Kat?"

"I imagined he might have kidnapped Kat so he could have her to himself. In fact, that morning when I saw her empty bed I thought he had taken her, but when she never showed up—and hasn't since … well, obviously Cody doesn't have her. He's still pretty depressed about it and hasn't been the same since. On weekends when he has Tempest all she says is how sad he is. So clearly it wasn't him. It had to be someone else. As for who, I hoped the police would have figured that out by now."

"What about Scott, your boyfriend at the time?"

"No, Scott would never hurt Kat. He was an amazing father. Had a son—two actually. Though the oldest is in the Air Force down in Florida right now. The younger one, Mikey, lived with us most of the time. A sort-of shared custody deal, but the mom … well, you know how those things go. It's never simple."

I drew Helen's attention to subtle details at the time of Kat's disappearance. Had she ever noticed an unfamiliar vehicle parked down the street? She couldn't remember. Had she ever seen a stranger walking past their house? No one that stood out to her. During the day Kat was abducted, had anything unusual happened? It was too long ago to recall. Someone had to have seen something, but those details were long buried, too deep for me to unearth.

What really bothered me, though, was two people in her life, gone. Too much death tied back to this woman to simply ignore the coincidence.

"Why'd you and Scott split up?"

"It just got … hard after Kat went missing. I wasn't myself. Always angry. Always trying to pick a fight with him. He never treated me bad, and he understood why, but I just couldn't get past it. Things were … tainted after Kat was gone. Scott was a reminder of her. I wonder if he'd still be alive today if I hadn't broken up with him."

"Do you know why anyone would want to kill Scott?"

"No idea. He was a genuinely nice guy. Even his ex-wife couldn't say anything bad about him. Loved to go hunting with his uncle. Worked hard. Was even up for a promotion at work.”

“Where was that?”

“Drew’s Plumbing. Drew, his boss, loved Scott. Everyone did. He just had one of those easygoing personalities that you can’t help but like. I just can’t believe someone would want to kill him. Why?”

Her eyes searched mine. I looked away, discomfited. Tempest was still engrossed in *Frozen*. When I looked back at Helen, she was rising to show me to the door.

“Wish I could tell you more.” Helen sighed as I eased past her and gingerly placed the ball of my foot on the rotting steps. “So many whys,” she added dreamily. “Like, why don’t my sorry-ass neighbors help me with my yard? God, how I miss having a man around.”

There was a private ache in her voice, and I didn’t know quite what to say. “You have a nice day, Helen,” I muttered stupidly, following the path I’d made in the overgrown grass back to my car.

“You let me know if you find out anything, hear?” she called after me.

“I will.”

I had a suspicion about one why. Perhaps the killer knew something about Scott’s involvement in Kat’s disappearance. It would make sense if this was a vigilante killer. Of course I couldn’t tell Helen that and sully her memory of a man she clearly loved. But if I could find out who killed Scott, maybe the killer knew what happened to Kat.

Chapter 20

Two years ago ...

The metal bunk bed squeaked under the tiny tossing body of Kat Brannigan, the bed springs grumpy with age. As long as her little sister Tempest slept in their shared bedroom, the monsters stayed away and Kat snoozed soundly. But almost every night, as Tempest awoke and snuck into their mother's bed, Kat would find herself imagining all kinds of things, from possessed puppies to giant blue hairy monsters ... the latter inspired by the *Monsters Inc.* movies they watched. Tonight it was something trying to get through the window, scratching, clawing, scraping its way inside. Her instinct warned her to flee for the safety of her mother's bedroom, but the last time she'd done that her mother shooed her out with the threat of a spanking and no television for two days for waking her up.

Somehow Tempest was exempt from that rule, and no matter how much Kat protested that it wasn't fair, her mom just kept saying that Tempest didn't have kindergarten in the morning, so she could sleep in. Kat had to learn to be a big girl. She was five, after all.

A scratch along the windowpane jarred her upright as she peered into the dark trying to see what it was. Though she was petrified to make contact, her inquisitive nature overtook any sensibility. She watched in fearful silence as something ran its long claw across the screen, splitting the mesh in half. Her window was cracked open to let the cool night breeze in. Their single-wide didn't have the luxury of central air conditioning to fight off the unusually high temperatures of this North Carolinian spring. Even the pre-dawn air wafted in a sticky humidity that made her sweat.

From her upper bunk perch Kat watched the window for several long minutes, listening to the wind whistle through the trees outside. The shadows began moving, so she tossed her blanket over her head, hiding from whatever lurked outside. Closing her eyes, she began humming to herself a song her mother sang to her every night, a soothing rendition of Guns N' Roses' "Sweet Child O' Mine." As long as Kat didn't see whatever was out there, it couldn't see her, she reasoned.

As she curled into a safe little ball hidden by a My Little Pony bedspread, she heard a soft *thump,* then a brief silence before she felt one arm grab her waist and the other cover her mouth. She wriggled around to face him, finding a patch of faceless black beneath a hood.

"Shhh," a voice whispered. "I'm not going to hurt you. I found a stray kitten outside. You wan' to see 'im?"

But she was too scared to think about kittens when she could barely breathe.

"Hey, it's okay. Your mom said we could go on an adventure together, but I don't want you to be scared. She made me promise you wouldn' wake no one up. Are you up for an adventure—and we can take the kitten with us?"

Kat always did love new and exciting things. Especially when it involved cute, fluffy animals.

"But if we're goin' to do this, I need you to stay quiet. I even got some treats for you ... and something for the kitten too. You ready to play with 'im?"

Of course Kat wanted to play with the kitten. What kid wouldn't? She wanted to answer and worked her lips experimentally. But the big, sweaty hand wouldn't let her speak.

"If you're quiet, I'll let go of your mouth. Can you stay quiet like a little mouse?"

She nodded and gave a muffled "mmm hmm."

The arms pulled her against a long warm body but loosened around her face, then carried her to the window. "Look," the voice said, holding her over the window ledge.

Kat obediently peered out. A nearby security light shrouded the yard in pale light. Sure enough, there was a kitten. A tiny gray ball of soft purring cuteness. Its kissable head was buried in a can of tuna that Kat could smell all the way from where she looked down on him. She never did like that fishy smell and refused to eat tuna noodle casserole when her mom made it for supper in case a hint of tuna snuck through the mayonnaise and noodles. When the kitten looked up at her with bright yellow eyes, he meowed eagerly. Now she just *had* to pet him.

"Can I hold him?" Kat whispered.

"Sure. I'll carry you out."

But Kat wasn't so sure it was a good idea.

"I can't. I'll get in trouble."

"I promise you won't get in trouble. Your mom already said it was okay. Just for a little bit, though."

"Okay," Kat agreed warily.

Together they clambered out of the window, Kat held firmly under her arms as they angled themselves through the opening, then dropped down like two bags of flour on the wet ground. Picking up the kitten, she held him to her chest, planting kisses all up and down his head and belly while he purred contentedly.

"Time to go," the voice said. She felt the strong arms picking her back up. "You can bring your little friend with you."

And the fun ended there. As he swung her up under his arms, Kat squeezing the kitten and the man squeezing Kat, the hand resumed its firm grip against her mouth, the other arm hauling her sideways as she dangled helplessly, soundlessly, until they disappeared into the dark. As Kat clung to her furry companion, she wondered where they were going, why he held her so tightly that it hurt ... and then a single thought that grew bigger and larger and more frightening by the second: would she ever see her mom again?

No amount of kicking or flailing would free her. No amount of pleading would save her. As the man hauled her across the empty dirt road, no one saw their shadows slipping through the night.

Chapter 21
Ari

The guilt trip I had taken myself on was a bumpy ride. Every hour that I stayed silent was a tightening noose around my neck. Keeping secrets had never been my thing, eventually causing rifts that I'd spent a lifetime trying to mend. But sometimes the price of truth felt too high.

I hadn't yet told Tina about Giana. It wasn't like I wanted to hide it from her, or that I felt she shouldn't get her baby back, but I just couldn't push the image of that happy, perfect Baxter family from my head. It was the life every child dreamed of, all the love and affection in the world at her fingertips, not to mention the beautiful home and endless toy supply and probably a pony in her future, and she'd be exchanging it for a pale imitation—someone who couldn't even love herself. The question lingered, like a vulture lazily circling in the sky: how could Tina take care of a child when she couldn't even take care of herself?

Was it my call to hold back this dream of reuniting with her daughter from the only real friend I had?

Could I even call myself a friend at this point?

What was more important: a mother's justice or a child's well-being?

The questions volleyed in my head, making me dizzy and nauseous.

It was too grueling to think about right now. My eyelids blinked heavily, but my brain buzzed too much to sleep. For some reason a little girl named Kat Brannigan wandered into my thoughts, alone and abandoned, a cold case apparition. It wasn't my place to investigate her disappearance—I'd been warned to stay away—but I couldn't help it. Maybe the broken child inside of me urged me to keep searching for answers. Maybe it was losing Carli that motivated my empathy for the poor girl. Or maybe I just needed to see a child victim be avenged and her family given closure. It was why I went into this field anyway, wasn't it? I knew what a lack of closure felt like. No one deserved that.

How could Tristan ask me to sit by while this girl—alive or dead, no one knew for sure, though by now the worst-case scenario seemed most likely—continued to stay missing? She needed a final goodbye from the mother who still referred to her in the present tense. *"We call her Kat."* Helen still clung desperately to hope. After two years of no news, what harm could it possibly cause if I did a little research, put on my big-girl investigator pants?

I was smart. I was capable. I'd survived on my own despite a life of hell; its fire had tempered me, molded me into someone stronger, more durable. Able to handle a little cold-case missing child investigation.

Grabbing my handy-dandy case file notepad and pencil, I sat on my sofa scribbling notes of everything I knew after my talk with Helen. Kat had disappeared without a sound—no screams or cries. Helen had been asleep in bed with Scott, and sometime during the night Tempest had slipped in between them. It was only when Helen awoke that she found Kat's bed empty, window screen slit open, and no sign of her daughter. Her first call was to Cody, the most likely suspect. The second call was to the police.

There was always the possibility that Helen and Scott were behind Kat's disappearance. Framed the whole thing by slicing through the screen, staging every last detail. From the boot prints outside the house, to the smeared muddy tracks in Kat's room. It happened more often than not—children killed or sold by the parents' own hand. Just like Tina was.

Tristan had said much the same thing to me. But after questioning the couple, the police ended up letting them go, along with the search for answers. There simply wasn't enough manpower to hunt down the countless kids that went missing each day. Without evidence of—or witnesses to—an actual crime, they had to, as if the justice system shrugged its shoulders and moved on to the next victim.

I tried to visualize how the events unfolded. I didn't know who to believe, who to trust. Were there holes in Helen's testimony that I could chip at to get to the truth? While Tempest was supposedly sleeping in Helen's bed, where in the house was Mikey during Kat's abduction? After all, she'd said he was living with them too. With four other people in the house, wouldn't someone have seen something? Heard something? But the bigger question was would Helen or Scott really go to such efforts to stage the scene, to the point of actually climbing in through the window? And if so, and Helen knew Kat was dead, why would she refer to her as if she was still alive?

Unless there was another end game. If Helen sold her to sex traffickers, she'd still be alive somewhere out there … hopefully. That is, if Kat hadn't become another Marla Rivers.

Many rural low-income neighborhoods were known for being abduction hot-spots. Close to Interstate 95, a kidnapper could easily hop on the highway that led down the east coast, all the way to Florida. He could have crossed two state lines before Kat had woken up. That is, assuming he hadn't killed her first.

The warnings to keep a close eye on your kids, lock your doors at night, inform your children about stranger danger—they weren't for nothing. Evil was real. So prevalent, in fact, that drugged-up abductors were now venturing out in broad daylight in public areas for their snatch-and-runs. While Mom loaded groceries into her minivan in the grocery store parking lot, kidnappers were stealing children from their car seats before Mom knew what happened. It was a scary world, but my job was to make it a little bit safer by putting one villain at a time behind bars. Give 'em something to be afraid of—that's what I wanted to do. Scare those bastards straight.

My parents had often said I loved a challenge as a child. Some things never change.

Having solved the mystery of Giana's location—without Battan's help—I felt invigorated, confident in my PI skills, and was left with a Kat-Brannigan-size hole to pour my energy into, other than filing paperwork at the precinct. My hands were tied from working the connection between Battan and Marla's death; Tristan had everything he needed, now that he'd gotten his hands on the ledger, and with Tina's witness testimony, he was a few interrogations away from finding out who N. Bledsoe was, the name behind the $10,000 payment around the time of Marla's death. Maybe finding out what happened to Kat, giving her family closure, was exactly what I needed to do to satiate my craving to save the world.

What could it hurt if I poked around a little bit?

Chapter 22
Ari

Learning the fine art of interrogation techniques was on next semester's course load. But it didn't mean I couldn't practice now.

Besides Kat's mother Helen, and the murdered stepfather Scott, who obviously would be of no use, the next best person to talk to was Kat's father, Cody Brannigan. If anyone had his own anger-fueled suspect list—or in my theory should be on it—it was the bio-dad. Tristan had mentioned his domestic violence history. All with the same woman, his then-wife Helen. I hadn't expected his arrest record to be two pages long, a grade A wife-beating douche bag. Certainly he'd been one of Tristan's prime suspects, but after several uneventful interrogations and surveillance that led nowhere, he became a dead end as far as the captain was concerned. After checking the database at work for his last known address and poring over the case file notes, I clocked out for the day and headed straight to Cody Brannigan's house on the outskirts of Raleigh.

The townhouse he lived in sat in the middle of a line of average homes on an average street. All matching gray aluminum siding; the only difference from one to another was the color of the front door or faux shutters, all dismally bland shades of blue, black, and brown, with the occasional burgundy. Clearly the Home Owner's Association ruled with an iron fist in this neighborhood.

I had to parallel park half a mile down the street, which took me over ten minutes as I inched my way back and forth between two huge SUVs that parked so crookedly that they deserved to get dented. I never had the luxury of a father teaching me the nuances of parallel parking as a teen, but coaxing my tiny car between these two would have challenged even the most expert parking valet.

Walking along the tree-lined sidewalk, I passed a young mother—she looked close to my age, in her mid-twenties—pushing a baby in a stroller, and I wondered what it would be like to be her. To have a family. To spend time with my kids. To watch them grow. To come home to a husband and a noisy house.

Maybe that last part was the problem—I'd always want to be the one coming home, not the one someone else was coming home to. Sitting at home all day, entertaining little kids? Fuhgettaboutit. How did mothers do it without losing their sanity? It sounded boring as hell. But then again, what man would want to marry a woman who felt the way I did about domestic life?

Watching the house numbers roll downward, I found the address I was looking for, shiny gold numerals emblazoned against a black door. I pressed a dimly lit doorbell button and heard the chime inside, a standard melody used by millions of other doorbells. A man answered the door, his head so shiny and bald I wanted to rub it for good luck. I noticed the twin eagle claw tattoos on either side of his thick neck, like talons clutching his collar. He had kind brown eyes and a nice smile, which defied what his arrest record told me.

"Good evening, miss. Can I help you?" he asked pleasantly. Was this polite man the same one who beat his wife once upon a time? I supposed the best of killers were the most charming ones. Ones who could easily draw victims in.

"I'm looking for Cody Brannigan."

"Look no more. You've found him."

"Oh, hi. My name is Ari Wilburn, and I'm with the Durham Police Department. May I come in for a moment?" I didn't want to mention that my job as a file clerk had absolutely nothing to do with why I was there. I figured sliding around those details was the only way he would speak to me. I'm sure it was illegal impersonating an officer, though was it really impersonation if I didn't say I was a police officer? The devil was in the details.

His smile faded away. "Oh God. You've found my daughter Kat. Is she—?"

Watching my face carefully, he stepped aside for me to slide past him inside the entryway.

"No, sir. I'm informally investigating her disappearance—off the books. The department doesn't know I'm here." I needed to cover my ass just in case this conversation ever came up with my boss. "I've been going through old files and came across Kat's. I figured maybe I could offer a fresh look at what happened, if you're willing to talk to me."

He turned toward the living room, talking with his back to me. "Yeah, sure. Why not? I'm surprised after all this time they've even kept the file. After so much time passes, you kind of give up hope that anyone cares, y'know?"

"The department is doing everything they can to get answers, sir."

"Cody. You can call me Cody."

"Okay, thanks, Cody. I'm sorry that we haven't found your daughter yet, but I'm hoping to change that."

The living room was unremarkable, save for its

messiness. Brown suede matching sofa and loveseat, two end tables covered with random papers and fragments of children's toys. A coffee table littered with empty plates, mugs, and cereal bowls indicated Cody—and Tempest, when he exercised his visitation rights—took their meals here, before the shrine of a wall-mounted flat-screen TV. The only notable personal effect was a family portrait on the wall of Cody, Helen, Kat, and Tempest in happier days. The picture looked to have been professionally, if rather gaudily, framed. The Olan Mills logo stood out against the black background. I imagined what an event it must have been for the family, dressing up in their Sunday best to get their portrait taken in a "fancy" studio.

"Coffee or anything?" he offered, still standing while I took a seat on one end of the sofa. A sharp object poked at the back pocket of my jeans. Scooting aside, I pulled a Snow White mini-figure out from between the cushions, finding a puzzle piece and a board game token along with it. Sofas tended to hide a trove of childhood treasures, though the days of finding loose change like when I was a kid were long gone since the advent of debit cards.

"No thanks. I won't stay long. I just need to ask a few questions."

Cody sat on the farthest end of the loveseat. His right leg bounced uncontrollably with a nervous tremor he seemed unaware of. "Okay, shoot."

"I understand you and Helen are divorced. What happened there?"

"Typical marriage problems, I guess. I didn't like what she did for a living, and I felt she'd be better off staying home with the girls. She disagreed. And we were stuck at an impasse that we couldn't get past."

So we were going to start off being evasive ... I'd have my work cut out for me.

"Ah, the bartending, right?" Cody nodded. "I can see

your perspective. She probably got hit on a lot, and no husband wants to watch his wife be sexualized by other men—especially when she's the mother of his children."

"See? You get it. I don't know why it was so difficult for her to understand. But it's water under the bridge now."

I'd gained his confidence. Time to hit him with a sucker punch. "Full disclosure here—Helen told me violence was common in your marriage."

"Of course she did." Cody exhaled loudly and dropped his elbows on his knees, resting his face on his hands. "Yes, Helen and I had our fair share of fights. Though I wasn't the one who started it. If you look at my record, I have no history of violence before Helen. All my problems started after I married her. The reality? She'd beat on me, and when I tried to defend myself she'd call the cops on me. Of course they always sided with her, the woman. Because the woman's always the victim. No one ever considers the man a victim."

"Cody, c'mon now. You're bigger, stronger, easily able to walk away from a fight. And if she was beating you, why were you so intent on staying married to her?"

"First of all, I love my wife—I'm sorry, my ex-wife. No matter what she did to me, I always loved her. And she was a great mom. So I figured it was better to deal with her breakdowns than to lose her altogether. And as for walking away from a fight, have you met my wife? She's what you might call a big-boned gal—not fat, just meaty in an attractive way. I like curves on a woman." He looked my slender frame over appraisingly and added, "No offense."

"None taken." Well, maybe a *little*.

"And she's taller than a lot of men. Hell, she's probably stronger than me, too. She doesn't take any crap from anybody. But walking away was not an option, because she liked the confrontation. To be honest, I think ignoring her would have made her even angrier."

"Is that why you shaved your head—to appear more menacing?"

"Premature balding, actually. Thanks for questioning my manhood, by the way." He grinned, and I couldn't help but feel bad for him now. "And in case you were wondering, the tattoo isn't a stick-on. It's real … and yes, it makes me feel more manly."

I laughed. At least all of his suffering—losing his child, his wife, his good-guy image—hadn't stolen his sense of humor.

"Sorry. I wasn't trying to emasculate you. It's just, well, a red flag when a girl goes missing and you find a history of violence from the father—plus a divorce on top of that. Logically it makes the most sense that you would have taken her, considering your wife was seeking primary custody. Run away with her, start a new life, but then why not Tempest too?" I examined him, searched his eyes for the truth, saw the wrinkles of worry and the paleness of sleepless nights. I sensed that he'd lost himself when he lost Kat. "But I'm thinking that's not what happened."

Sitting back, he crossed the bouncing leg over the other, hands folded in his lap. "You actually believe I'm innocent. Why? The cops certainly didn't."

"Because I know the look of someone who's lost the other half of their heart. Kat was yours, wasn't she?"

"Yeah, I guess you could say that."

"What kind of relationship did you have with her?"

His eyes watered in the wistful, contemplative way when sepia memories come alive again in vibrant color.

"Kat was funny. Oh, her sense of humor was far more advanced even than mine." He grinned boyishly. "And smart. Whip-smart. By eighteen months she knew her entire alphabet. By two she was spelling words. She would have gone on to do great things if she was still here. And beautiful. Dimpled cheeks, eyes that unveiled your secrets—she was intense, in a good way. That kind of intensity that makes you want to be a better man because you know she deserves so much more than you can offer. And yet she was so perfectly happy with the simple life she was given. She was my everything."

It was as if he was reciting a lovely, poetic epitaph at her funeral. His body still mourned her in the stoop of his shoulders, the creases in his forehead, the grief in his voice. Perhaps every day he relived his own personal memorial for his daughter.

"How are things with your other daughter, in spite of everything that happened?"

A smile softened the sadness in his face. He looked away from me, toward the family portrait on the wall, then returned his gaze to me. "Don't get me wrong, I love Tempest. But it's ... well, I never had the connection with Tempest that I had with Kat. Kat always loved me most, a daddy's girl. Tempest is her mama's little girl. But she's still my sun, moon, and stars. She's all I got left. I miss Kat with every fiber of my being, but Tempest ... well, she keeps me sane. I've always loved both my girls. I would never hurt them. Ask Helen—even though she hates me, she knows I'd never hurt my girls."

I believed Cody wouldn't, but what about Helen?

"Would she ever hurt them?"

Cody waved his hands frantically. "God, no! She's a great mother. I don't blame her for what happened. I don't think she had anything to do with it."

"What about Scott Guffrey, her boyfriend at the time?"

"No, I can't imagine him wanting to hurt Kat. I mean, why? He's a father himself. I knew the guy—he was a good guy from good stock. No, like I told the cops, I think it was the drug dealer who lived down the road from Helen. I've heard it happens—those people stealing kids and selling them for ..." Closing his eyes, he shook his head. "I can't even think about that. My baby girl ... that happening to her. The cops might have questioned him, I don't remember, but they didn't go anywhere with it."

"Do you have his name?"

"No, just what he looks like and where he lives ... if he still lives there."

It sounded like a wild-goose chase to me. But one I was willing to pursue just in case there was something to it.

"If you give me whatever information you have, I'll look into it."

It was a shot in the dark, I knew, since Kat would have been long gone by now if the dealer had sold her. And it wasn't like he would just blurt out a confession simply because I asked him to. But maybe I could find something, anything, that would point me in the right direction. For the sake of this shattered family, I was willing to do just about anything.

Chapter 23

Tears. Screams. Violence. Rebellion. Anger. Hate. Love. Passion.

Welcome to the other side of existence. The dark side that turns everyday people into killers. What makes an average person decide it's okay to take a life? Or it's okay to avenge the dead?

I've learned a lot about those urges, those feelings that awaken the darkest primal side of us. It's where humanity dies and the animal takes over. I hated that side, and yet here I was embracing it. I didn't know why. I just do, act, react to the thing that compels me. To me, it was justice of the highest order. A calling.

Of course there's always that one person who unwittingly gets in the way of the hero. Their intentions are good, but it puts everyone at risk. Such people must learn to butt out. Such people must be culled.

Why? Why must some people push, push, push?

I'd been following Ari Wilburn to learn more about her, only to discover her mocking me with an endless quest for answers. Why couldn't she just accept things and let it go? As she threaded together the details of what happened with Scott, with Kat, with Jackson—she was climbing a rope that would lead to me. That same rope would eventually hang me.

She was a rebel like me, and while I respected her for

that, it also would end up getting someone killed. She was putting herself in the line of fire, and I didn't know how many warning shots it would take to get her to back off.

It didn't help that people like Ari Wilburn and me—the bruised, broken souls raised on pain and self-sufficiency—didn't care enough about life to worry about losing it. So my threats would likely prove fruitless.

Unless ... unless I threatened someone she loved. There weren't many people in that category, at least from what I could gather by watching her. Her mother and father, maybe. A detective love interest that I'd seen coming and going from her place numerous times. Then a girl, a pretty Latino girl. Rough around the edges, but interesting. I found myself watching her long after Ari had left her apartment. The blond tips of her short black hair stuck messily in all directions, which I found cute. Some of the mail delivered to the apartment—which I'd clandestinely examined, naturally—was addressed to Tina Alvarez. I slid her name into my memory bank for safekeeping. I might need it for later.

Then there was a family in that rich section of Durham, with two little kids. Philip and Eve Baxter, I discovered after a property records search. Ari had only lurked outside their house, never approaching them. Perhaps it was time I made an introduction. I didn't want it to come to that—hurting kids, it should never come to that—but I needed to make a point before my neck was on the chopping block courtesy of Durham's boys in blue.

The loss of a few innocents was worth the bigger cause. Or as Mr. Spock so aptly put it, "The needs of the many outweigh the needs of the few."

One last warning shot. I'd give Ari that. Then it was war.

Chapter 24
Ari

If you've ever seen *Breaking Bad,* imagine Walter White's sidekick, Jesse Pinkman. When I knocked on the door of dilapidated trailer number six, that was who answered the door—that is, a poor man's version of the character. Yeah, I have to admit, I found Jesse kind of hot; Andrew Watson wasn't. He favored Jesse enough around the face to draw the comparison, but he lacked his brooding sexiness—and hard body. Andrew was shirtless, of course, in keeping with some arcane law peculiar to redneckdom that dictates its members practice upper body nudity whenever possible. His skinny chest was hairless and ghostly pale like it'd never been exposed to sunlight before.

"Hey, pretty thang."

He smiled down at me about a foot below him on the stoop, his teeth brown from either too much Red Man tobacco or meth use. One skinny arm hung lazily at his hip; he flexed the bicep of the other in a bizarre trailer trash attempt at seduction. Instead I wanted to vomit.

"Hi. I'm looking for Andrew Watson. Does he live here?"

"Andrew? I ain't been called that since my grandmama was yellin' that for me wearing shorts to church. It's Andy.

And yeah, this is my place. You wanna cum inside? You git my meaning?" He laughed at his own crude innuendo.

"Um." How deep was too deep for me to go when trying to get answers? Something told me Andy was a take first, ask for permission later kind of guy. "I won't be long. I just wanted to know if you knew the family down the street—Helen and Scott. They had three kids, two girls and a boy."

His smile faded. "Sure, I know 'em. Scott owes me money. Tell 'im I'm comin' to collect."

"For what?" I don't know why I asked, because I doubted he would give me a truthful answer.

"Let's just say I helped him out when he was going through a rough patch. Helped him feel better, y'know? How about you—need a little pick-me-up?"

"No thanks." I smiled stiffly. "But I know who to come to if I do. So you've done business with Scott?"

"Only a few times—just some special K and pot. Well, anyway, dude never paid me for his last fix."

"That *dude* is dead," I said flatly.

"Really? Aw shit. I ain't ever gonna see my money, am I?"

"So you didn't know Scott was murdered?"

"What, you a cop or something?"

"Do I look like a cop to you?" I winked, propping my hand on my hip, unsure why I even did that. Maybe to throw him off. Or maybe to prove something to myself, that I could get this guy to talk. I didn't know what it would take, but Andy knew something and wasn't telling.

"Ain't never met a cop as fine as you."

"Aw shucks. Don't make me blush. Look, I'm just trying to see if anyone who knew him might know what happened to him. Like, who killed him."

"Nah, I ain't seen him for months."

"How about the rest of the family that lived there? Did you know them?"

"Nope. I seen little kids running around before, but I don't pay much attention."

"So you wouldn't know anything about the little girl who was abducted from their home about two years ago?"

"Two years ago? I can't even remember what I did last night. Oh wait—yeah, I do remember. I did some girl named Candi!"

I realized then that Andy played as dumb as he looked. This guy had nothing of value to offer me. I was antsy to leave.

"So you didn't know about the kidnapping? How could you not have known? There were cops crawling all over this place. Asking neighbors. I'm sure they came here to ask if you'd seen anything."

Dropping his arm, he rested it on the doorknob, clearly as anxious to get rid of me as I was to slap that nasty mouth of his.

"Lady, I don't know what you're gittin' at, but I ain't got nothing to do with any of that. I was in jail two years ago, so if you think I have anything to do with some kid gittin' stolen, do your research first. Unless you wanna bang, I suggest you take your hot ass off my front porch."

I couldn't get away from this jerk fast enough. As I left, I wondered if Cody knew Andy had an alibi for the night of Kat's disappearance. Had he purposely sent me down a dead end? And if so, why?

Chapter 25
Ari

"Welcome to Great Clips. How can I help you?" The receptionist was almost too pretty as she smiled up at me from behind a marbled Formica reception desk. Extreme makeup from the sparkly purple eye shadow to the red lips framed in black lip liner. Hair curled and upswept like she was going to prom. Yet somehow for her it worked. Me? I'd look like a clown—the scary kind from Stephen King's *It*. Though, what other kind of clown was there?

"I was hoping to get a haircut with Lillian Guffrey? Is she working today?"

It had taken a bit of good old-fashioned sleuthing to find out that Lillian wasn't home today and that she worked at Great Clips as a hairdresser. That was the useful thing about bored shut-in neighbors—they often knew everyone else's business and were happy to share it with anyone who knocked on their doors. As I headed to the North Pointe salon, I figured I could use a trim anyway, so what better opportunity to talk to Lillian than when her guard was down while at work. Hairdressers were notorious gossips, too. I'd have her eating out of my hand.

"As a matter of fact, she has an opening now, if you're ready."

Tra-la-la. Things were going my way today.

"Perfect. Thanks."

After being seated in a swiveling salon chair in front of a floor-to-ceiling mirror, Lillian Guffrey greeted me. Her mane of blond and gray curls was the first thing I noticed. Skimming the collar of her black smock, the unruly locks almost tempted me to get a perm for myself. A throwback to the 1990s era when Mariah Carey made it look good, before my time. I had a vague memory of my mom's attempt at a Julia Roberts look-alike, with her red hair permed big and bold. I had only been maybe five at the time, but she'd taken me with her to the beautician and we got our hair done together. I cried the entire time. After that, Mom always trimmed my hair herself—except for that one time I cut my own bangs. Let's just say Mom didn't order school pictures that year, but we never forgot my half-inch-long bangs job, and the scissors would forever remain hidden after that.

As Lillian and I discussed my hair prospects—"just a trim," I emphasized at least three times, because in hairdresser-speak a trim could be anywhere from an inch off to half a foot—we made small talk about her grandkids, hobbies, and eventually I segued into my job at the police department.

"Guffrey is your last name?" I asked her. My acting skills weren't half bad. "We just had a case for a Scott Guffrey. Any relation to you?"

Her busy fingers slid out of my hair, setting the scissors down on the small table next to her. Pushing my chair around to face her, she looked at me. Oh crap. I had blown my cover.

The cheerfulness had left her voice. She spoke now in a flat monotone. "He's my son. Was. Was my son. I'm guessing you know that he was murdered."

"Yes, I'm so sorry." That part wasn't an act. The lady

was as sweet as apple pie.

"Do you know anything about the case? I keep calling to see if the police have any idea who did it, but so far nothing."

"If you give me your number, I'd be happy to stay in touch if there's any new developments."

"I appreciate that," she said.

"How are your grandkids handling the loss of their father?"

"Mikey's taking it the hardest. He's only five, just started kindergarten this year. The older one, Kevin, he's hanging in there. Though I don't see him, so I can't really say. He's all grown. In the military." She handed me a framed certificate of achievement with Kevin Guffrey's name on it. "Graduated with honors. A genius. Amazing kid with a full scholarship offer to Duke. But he wanted to serve his country. With his intelligence, they suggested he'd make an excellent explosive ordnance disposal specialist. That's a fancy way of saying defusing bombs. Isn't that amazing?" Her face brightened as she bragged about her grandson. The flush of pride looked good on her.

"Where's he now?"

"Stationed in Florida. He calls to check in when he can, but I'm sure he's busy with all the training and whatnot down there. With Scotty gone, I hardly ever see Mikey anymore. His mother, Candace, never brings him around, though she and I have never had a ... well, amicable relationship to begin with. It was always a big drama anytime I wanted to see my own grandkids."

"What do you mean?"

Pulling up a leather stool, she sat in front of me, grabbed a chunk of hair, and worked her way through the strands with a razor.

"Scotty had proposed to Candace after getting her

pregnant with Kevin, but she said no. He asked her again after Mikey came along. Still turned him down. She liked playing the field too much. I hate to just come out and say it, but Candace was a slut, seeing a different man every night. And she was a mother, to boot! Poor Scotty. She dragged his heart through the mud. She was a right awful witch, if you ask me. Mostly because of drugs and alcohol, but the sleeping around really broke his heart. Lost custody of the kids a while back due to the drug abuse and negligence, then used her feminine wiles to convince Scotty to share custody."

"Sounds like a piece of work."

Lillian leaned in slyly. "More than just that. I'm not one to gossip, but I just have to say I don't think it was coincidence when Scotty was killed. It was right after he was going after full custody of Mikey again. Candace couldn't shake the heroin and he didn't want that around Mikey. Shortly after he tells her this, he ends up dead. Doesn't that sound suspicious to you?"

Candace had left those details out during her interrogation. Could she have overpowered Scott? If she'd gotten him drunk as a skunk, she could have done just about anything. After all, the autopsy report showed a high blood-alcohol content and date rape drugs—which would have made him an easy victim. Which made me wonder if Scott and Jackson's deaths were truly linked. Could it be two different killers? Tristan was convinced it was the same person, but besides similar stabbing patterns, what else tied them together? The only way to find out was to keep digging deeper until I hit something solid.

I had to wonder: could Candace be behind both Scott's death and Jackson's?

"I'm curious, but how did you know about the behind-the-scenes stuff going on with Candace? Was this information coming from Scott?"

"Oh, honey, I have ways of keeping tabs on that little snake. I'm close friends with her next-door neighbor. She keeps me informed, because Lord knows Scotty would never tell me anything because he wanted to keep the peace. If he even knew the half of what that woman was capable of ..." She visibly shuddered.

"Did you tell the police what you've told me?"

"Of course, but Candace denied it. Said I made it up to make her look bad because of our family feud."

Perhaps Candace had a relationship with Jackson. Lillian seemed like the type to know what went on behind Candace's closed doors.

"Does the name Jackson Jones ring a bell with you?"

Placing her finger on her lips, she contemplatively turned her head sideways. "Why does that name sound familiar? Was he in the news for something?"

"Another murder victim. Possibly tied to Scott. I was wondering if maybe Candace was sleeping with him."

"I never got the names of her *beaus*—if you want to call them that. It was a revolving door, so if Candace had anything to do with Jackson's death and starts killing off everyone she's ever slept with, well, you're going to have a victim list a mile long."

Lillian was now describing every detective's worst nightmare.

Chapter 26
Ari

If there was one thing I hated about PI work, it was the driving. It was a time suck. And then the surveillance part … boring. It took some imagination, but I'd eventually found ways to entertain myself during those parts of the job, like expanding my karaoke repertoire and mastering Sudoku.

By the time I'd gotten done with my haircut—Lillian did a smashing job; I found myself admiring the new layered look in my rearview mirror while I searched on my phone's web browser for an address for Candace Rhoades, currently my top suspect in Scott's murder—it was early evening. I was too impatient to wait until tomorrow to speak with Scott's baby-mama-ex, especially since I'd have to wait until after work. I'd already postponed dinner plans with Tristan two nights in a row, so I didn't want to make it a third. I ached for some cuddles with my sexy chef boyfriend.

Besides, it would be a school night for little Mikey, so there was a good chance Candace would be home.

Thirty minutes later I pulled up to a cute little yellow brick home up on a hill. I climbed the stairs to the front door and knocked. A little boy answered, sporting a head of black curly hair that was the spitting image of his mother's, I realized, when she followed him to the door.

"Can I help you?"

The telltale ravages of heroin addiction showed on her face. She had a starved, emaciated look, like a ghoul deprived of dead bodies to feast upon. The pupils were pinpoints in lifeless, staring eyes. Her skin was ashen; there were fresh sores from incessant picking at the itchy skin, and scars and scabs from old wounds. The thin lips had an unsettling bluish tint. As I regarded her with mingled pity and curiosity, she crossed her arms across Mikey's chest and pushed the door halfway shut with the toe of her shoe, warily holding it in place. I knew I'd have to up my game as a budding PI to get anywhere with someone this damaged and guarded.

"My name is Ari Wilburn, and I'm with the Durham Police Department. I'd like to speak with Candace Rhoades. I'm assuming that's you?"

Shifting her weight, she looked at me with obvious annoyance. "Yeah, that's me. What's this about?"

I glanced down at Mikey. "I'm not sure you'll want him hearing this."

"Did I do something wrong?"

"No, ma'am, nothing at all. It's about Scott Guffrey. We might have a lead and I wanted to speak with you about it. See if you had any input on it."

She nudged Mikey aside. "Go watch television, bud."

"May I come in for a moment?"

"Do you have a warrant?"

I leaned in to whisper. "I, uh, I'm on my period right now and really need to change my pad. I'm so sorry to ask, but I'm petrified I'm leaking. I just want to use your bathroom, if that's okay."

"Oh, honey, sure." She stepped into the narrow entryway and pointed to a hallway that led past one door on each side. "Bathroom's at the end of the hallway. I have extra pads if you need one."

"You're a lifesaver," I said, giving her forearm an appreciative squeeze.

Women stuff I would have told Tristan if he was here. Sometimes it took a woman to get through to another woman.

I headed to the bathroom, slowing my pace as I passed the open doorways—both leading to bedrooms. The sparse one had a few toys and a mattress on the floor with a Batman comforter. Mikey's room. The other room across the hall was trashed with clothes, makeup, and God knows what else. Must be Candace's. Glancing back, Candace had disappeared into the belly of the house, so I slipped into her bedroom for a quick look-see. On top of her only piece of furniture, a large dresser, was a picture of Scott, whom I recognized from the autopsy photos, clad in camouflage and holding up a dead deer by its antlers. An older man with a mustache stood next to him. Behind them was a log cabin surrounded by woods. Its rustic appeal was lost on me, a city girl at heart.

The musty fragrance of wet earth, the pungent ripeness of rustling leaves, certainly all of it was invigorating in a Thoreau-esque "I went to the woods because I wished to live deliberately" sort of way. But I'd take the wafting smell of street vendor cheesesteak or the lemon polish scent of the inside of a mall any day. I wondered why a picture of the man she didn't want to marry, the man who threatened to take her children from her, was propped in full display in her bedroom.

With a final glance around the room, nothing else struck me as noteworthy, so I slipped into the bathroom before making my way back down the hall toward the living room where Candace tidied up food wrappers and colorful kindergartener drawings.

"Your son is a good artist," I said, picking up a child's depiction of a cabin surrounded by trees and handing it to her while she gathered a stack full.

"Thanks. Takes after his dad. Scott was always good at the artsy stuff."

She deposited the trash in a dented metal Durham Bulls garbage can and plunked the drawings down on a badly cracked vinyl ottoman. She raked crumbs and wads of lint off the baby-shit green sofa with her forearm—she wore long sleeves, I noticed, no doubt to hide her track marks—and beckoned me to sit. I did; she chose a decrepit wingback chair opposite me.

"Was he pretty hands-on with the kids?" She didn't know I knew about their custody battle and family drama. How honest would she be?

"Yeah, he was great with them. We worked hard to make sure we raised them together. Family has always been most important to us both."

Lie number one. I knew Lillian would have disagreed with Candace's outlook on family togetherness.

"Would you say you and Scott had a friendly relationship?"

"Absolutely. We've always gotten along."

Lie number two. I needed to start poking some holes.

"I heard that he could be somewhat unfair. That he had threatened to take the kids from you. How did that make you feel?"

"What? Who said that?" she demanded, her tone flustered. "Was it Lillian? That woman hates me and will say anything to make me look bad. No, you've got it all wrong. Scott and I mighta had a disagreement here and there—tell me what couple don't—but we both agreed that it was best the kids be in both of our lives. It's always healthiest to have a mom and dad, don't you think?"

"Absolutely, Candace. I didn't have either of my parents when I was growing up since I was in foster care." Maybe a little empathy could go a long way with Candace.

Perhaps my openness would help prompt her own. "In fact, I often thought about punishing my parents for sending me away. So you're telling me Scott never tried to file for full custody? Because I saw some legal documents that suggested he had."

"Okay, that—" Candace paused, avoiding eye contact as she searched the room for some explanation I would buy, then sighed defeat. "That was during a particularly hard point in my life." She tiptoed around the words like she was avoiding landmines. "But we both ended up agreeing that it wasn't best for anyone. As long as I got better, we'd keep the same shared custody arrangement we'd had for years. You can look it up—it's all in that legal file."

"Wow, I'm sorry to hear he did that to you. So you've never thought about punishing Scott for trying to take your kids from you?"

Her eyes narrowed on me. I felt her assessment as she weighed her reply. "No, I've never thought of hurting Scott. Was I pissed? Yeah. But enough to hurt him? No."

"How about your family—did they like him?"

"Oh yeah. Everyone liked Scott. He had that charming personality that sucks you in. My mama always wanted him as the son she never had. Hell, even my uncle liked him. The two went hunting together for years, even when we broke up. Best friends, practically."

The mustached man in the picture.

"Why didn't you two ever marry? It seems you liked him enough, and clearly he liked you enough to have two kids with you."

She coughed lightly, then glanced away, her wringing hands making me anxious. "Eh, I've never been the marrying type. I loved him, for sure, but we were different people. He wanted more kids, I didn't. He was dyin' to have a little girl. Our first, Kev, he was an accident 'cause we were young and reckless. Neither of us was ready. But with Mikey, Scott was over the moon when he found out we were having another baby. After that I was done. But no, Scott wanted us to keep popping out babies until we had a girl. That's when I realized nope, we weren't meant to be. Two boys were enough for me. Have you ever raised a boy?"

I shook my head. "No kids."

"Good for you. Enjoy the freedom while it lasts. Boys are a handful and suck up every ounce of energy you have. Anyway, we split and luckily he found Helen and it worked out."

It felt like a fishing expedition in a dry pond, but I had to ask. "Have you ever heard of anyone by the name of Jackson Jones?"

I watched her expression carefully, hoping she'd give some sign of recognition. Instead I saw nothing but genuine curiosity.

"No, sorry. That name don't ring a bell. Why? Who is he?"

"He was murdered last month. We think it may be tied to Scott's murder."

"Oh. He'd never mentioned anyone named Jackson, but it wasn't like I kept close tabs on who he hung out with after we split up."

"Were you aware that Scott and Helen had broken up before he was killed?"

"Yeah, he told me about it after that poor li'l girl Kat went missing. I can't even imagine going through something like that—losing a child. Scott was pretty messed up afterward."

"Do you think Scott had anything to do with Kat's disappearance?"

"You shittin' me? Scott loved kids, never even spanked ours. I can't see him hurting a child, especially a little girl.

I mean, he *really* adored Kat, the daughter he always wanted. Made Mikey a bit jealous, actually, just how much attention Kat got."

I was amazed at how cooperative Candace was being. Just as I was wondering how long it would last, it ended. She'd been a little fidgety during the interview, her gnawed fingernails—freakishly blue, like her lips—picking casually at her facial sores, but otherwise remarkably composed. Suddenly her eyes roved suspiciously around the room, as if searching for hidden microphones and cameras. Then they lighted on me. She seemed to see me for the first time and regarded me with cold malice, like someone about to hit a cockroach with a rolled-up newspaper.

"I think I've said all I care to say to you, young lady," she said, springing up from her chair. She tugged viciously at her bird's nest hair, pulling out a handful that she let float to the floor. "Scott didn't kill nobody, I didn't kill nobody. How dare you come strutting in here all high and mighty making your accusations!"

"Candace, I—"

"Out, just get the hell out of my house, and don't come back!"

She pushed the front door open and I breezed past her through it. A stream of paranoid invective followed me to the car. She was still in the doorway, gesticulating wildly and screeching as I peeled off.

Can you say "scary as shit sudden withdrawal episode"?

Heading home, I reflected on what I'd learned. Candace believed Scott's innocence, but I wasn't sure I did. More concerning was how she sugarcoated their relationship, slipping half-truths in every chance she got. Was this liar capable of killing Scott? Perhaps. But Jackson too? Doubtful. The precision, timing, planning, organization ... it was too complex for a junkie. Something felt wrong, so very wrong about all of this. While I didn't have answers yet, I sensed I was close. I knew Scott had to be connected to Kat's abduction, and that put him on a killer's radar. It was the only thing that made sense, especially if the serial killer was targeting child predators.

My father was connected to Marla's murder.

Scott was connected to Kat's disappearance.

That left Jackson's hidden sins.

Maybe once I uncovered Jackson's indiscretion it would lead me to the person tied to all three. The person who would keep killing until I stopped him—or her.

Chapter 27

Two years ago ...

Kat's question was muffled by the palm across her mouth, first to silence her and second to keep her still for the first several minutes of their bouncy drive over potholes and ruts, along empty black pastures and through the dense tree-lined forest. Looking up at her captor, she begged him with her eyes to let go.

"Will you behave if I remove my hand?" the driver asked.

She nodded.

"Good girl."

He released her.

"Where are we going?"

Her eyes were wide and curious with a naiveté that melted him into a pool of guilt.

"We're taking a short trip to go camping. How's that sound?"

"I wanna go home. I'm tired."

"We'll be there shortly, I promise."

After dumping a bag of snacks in Kat's lap, they bumped along the road in a rusted blue pickup truck for what felt like hours, until Kat finally dozed off. When the man nudged her awake, they were parked in front of a scary-looking cabin hidden in shadows and tucked between *Wizard of Oz*-ian trees full of gnarly cankers and knotholes. To Kat they had faces that looked like they wanted to eat her alive.

"I'm scared," Kat said to the man.

"There's nothing to be scared of. The forest is full of deer and bunnies and owls ... all kinds of cute, furry critters."

"I like deer. Tastes good too. Especially deer jerky."

"Me too. I love deer jerky."

"Where are we?"

"We're where you're gonna be living for a little while. It's somewhere magical, enchanted. You'll be like Snow White here."

"What about my mommy?"

"You'll see your mommy again soon. This is just for a short while. But I have a surprise for you. You'll love it, I promise. Let's go inside."

The man held her small warm hand as he led her inside the cabin, the door screeching in eerie protest as it opened. The smell of mildew hit them like a blow. Standing against a stone fireplace was a strange man, someone Kat had never seen before. He had two upper teeth with a big space between them, and two lower teeth flush together, so that when he smiled he displayed a neat row of rotten pickets. Kat gazed upon him in fascinated terror. He worked a wad of tobacco in his mouth. An oily black stream of viscous liquid oozed out of the corner of his mouth and dribbled down his chin. His voice sounded wet and gravelly.

"Hi, little girl. We're gonna have a fun time together."

"This nice man is going to watch over you for a short while, okay?"

"What? No, please, no! I wanna go home!" She didn't know where she was. She didn't know why. All she knew was that she did *not* want to spend a moment alone with that toothless stranger. Her cries became frantic, her screams louder as she clung to his legs. "Please take me back!"

As the man knelt down to calm her, Kat's hysteria unraveled into sobs. His eyes dampened with compassion. Pulling her into a hug, he held her head against his shoulder, running his hand down her bed-matted hair.

"You know what, let's just forget it and take you home." He leaned back from her, cupping her chubby cheeks in his hands. "This was a really bad idea and I'm not feeling good about it. You ready to go home?"

Kat nodded, a grateful smile showing through the whimpers.

"Hey, Norm," the man directed at Toothless, "I'm calling this off. You can keep the money, but I'm taking her home now."

Toothless shook his head slowly. "I don't think so."

Standing back up, the man turned to Toothless, his chest thrust out confrontationally.

"And what exactly are you going to do about it? This is emotional abuse, man, and it's also criminal. You'll still get your money, but I'm leaving with the girl."

Toothless clicked his tongue several times.

"See, I can't let that happen 'cause I already made plans. This little miss ain't goin' nowhere." Toothless eyed Kat with black soulless orbs that she was certain belonged to the monster in her nightmares. His hand rested on his back for the briefest of seconds, before he pulled out a gun and pointed it at Kat's temple. "Way I see it, she's worth a lot more than you're paying me if I sell her off."

The man stumbled backward at the sight of the gun, palms raised. "Let's keep a cool head, man. I said you could keep the money. You'd be getting paid to do nothing. Just let us go. Please, man."

Toothless cackled, syrupy spit spraying from his gapped mouth. "You don't get it. I already got a taker, everything already planned. Was gonna sell her right after you left. Git paid twice!" He let out a shrill whoop. "George'll love this one—she's purdy. And spunky. Little girls are valuable on the market these days. So how 'bout you hand her over so's I don't have to shoot ya dead?"

"Norm, please. Think about what you're doing," the man begged.

Two arms pulled Kat backward, behind the safety of legs. Just as Toothless cocked his gun, the door swung open again. Kat turned to look.

"Daddy!"

Chapter 28
Ari

The letter was sitting on my bed when I got home at dusk, my neatly tucked and smoothed bed. The only problem was that I couldn't remember the last time I'd made my bed.

The killer had broken into my apartment, which wasn't that impressive considering the complete lack of security and the broken lock on my first-story sliding glass door. The break-in wasn't what scared me the most. What sent a chill down my spine was that he placed the threat in my *bedroom*, where I slept, oblivious to the world, then took the time to meticulously make my bed. It was as if he was passing along the message *I am always watching, always waiting in the corners.* Nowhere was safe.

Worse yet, it wasn't just me he was after. When you grow up without parents sheltering you from the world's darkness, you learn methods of self-preservation. I'd gotten used to protecting myself. I'd done it all of my adolescence, defending myself against the system, against bullies, against the streets. But this threat was against Tina and Giana—an innocent *child*. Tina was already mentally fragile after all she'd gone through—losing both parents, albeit sucky horrible parents, and struggling with depression and anger after years of abuse. Anything more could break her soul beyond repair. The poor girl was barely an adult and had already endured a lifetime of the shittiest shit life had to offer.

Why Giana? Targeting a child to make a point? Coming from a so-called vigilante killer who murdered to avenge the lives of the innocent, this meant one thing: I was getting uncomfortably close and he was now backed into a corner. Fight or flight time. But he was too cowardly to face me himself, so he threatened the weak. A toddler and a young woman. I could find a way to keep Tina safe, but there was no way I could watch over Giana as well. Only Tristan could get me out of this mess I'd made.

I didn't want to draw a target on my friend's back or her daughter's family, but I could taste the end, touch it with my fingertips. It was possible I was one small clue away from figuring out who was behind Scott's murder, Jackson's sin against humanity, maybe even Kat's disappearance. Should I stop now? More than anything I wanted to keep pushing, but if it risked Tina or Giana's lives? No, I couldn't do that to them. But what about the killer's next targets? If I didn't figure it out soon, the killer would just keep killing.

This asshole obviously he didn't know much about me if he thought I'd roll over and play dead. But I knew I couldn't keep acting like some sort of comic book vigilante myself. Two heads were better than one, right? Maybe.

I picked up my cell phone and dialed.

"Hey, Tristan. I did something you're not gonna like, and now I need your help."

❧❧

"Damn it, Ari! I told you to stay out of it. You're dealing with a killer, not some peeping Tom. It's dangerous. Please listen to me for once."

I let Tristan rant and rave across from me on my living room sofa while I waited patiently for him to finish. I had propped my feet up on his lap like I usually did when we sat down to watch a movie together or just talk, but this time he nudged them away. This was a whole new level of anger I hadn't seen before. Slow burning but scalding hot. So I stayed quiet until I knew he'd finished his tirade. No point cutting him off before he'd had a chance to fully vent it all out.

"And now you've put Tina and Giana in danger because you can't stop poking around."

When it seemed like he'd run out of words, I took my turn to explain.

"First, I'm sorry. I know I'm not fully trained or whatever, and it's dangerous and all, but you've got to realize this is my passion. This is what I want to do with my life. My whole crappy upbringing shaped me for this kind of work. I'm tougher than I look, honey."

I squeezed his forearm, forcing him to feel me, to stay with me while I explained.

Tristan pulled his arm away, and my heart twinged just a little at the distance. "What about the people you've now put in danger?"

"Can't you offer police protection for them?"

"How the hell am I supposed to explain that to the Baxters? *Um, hey, family I don't know, my girlfriend is tracking a serial killer and led them straight to your door. So, I'll be having you watched until we catch this guy. Cool?* You can't just act like there's no consequences, Ari."

He poured the judgment on thick.

"So I'm just supposed to work in filing the rest of my life because some jerk wants to make me his puppet? No thanks!"

"That's not what I'm saying—"

But I wasn't even close to done yet. "I'm not some delicate flower you need to protect. I've taken care of myself for years, and I'm good at it. So telling me to stop being who I am—sometimes daring, sometimes hasty, but always me—isn't going to stop me. It'll just make me more stubborn."

"Is that even possible—you being more stubborn?" It was the first time he looked at me since he arrived at my apartment, and I caught the twinkle. Subtle, that azure spark of humor that cut through the tension.

"Oh, challenge accepted!" He returned my smile with a slight crease of his lip. I was close to breaking through the ice. "I really am sorry-not-sorry about getting involved, but I'm close, Tristan. I can feel it in my gut, y'know? I don't know how to explain it, but I must be right if he's resorting to threats now."

"I don't get it. You talked to all these same people I've already spoken to. Why the threat now? It's a safe assumption it's the same killer who murdered Scott and Jackson, and attacked your dad. We need to figure out what information you unearthed that caught his attention."

"I wish I knew. So you agree—I'm close. Really close. Right?"

"It would seem that way. But why did he—"

"Or she," I interrupted.

"—or *she* not threaten me when I questioned the same people two years ago?"

"He, she, whatever wasn't a killer back then. Scott was only murdered three months ago. Jackson only last month. I suspect this person is directly tied to Kat's abduction somehow, but two years ago they were innocent. Now they're not. This is about self-preservation."

"So give me a rundown of what you've found out. Let's compare notes."

"I haven't found out anything that you haven't, that's what's weird. My Spidey-sense tells me Scott had something to do with Kat's disappearance, since he was the serial killer's first target. Plus nine times out of ten it's someone close to the family." I remembered what Candace had said about Scott's desire for more kids—a girl in particular. "Scott's ex-girlfriend baby mama said he desperately wanted a little girl. Maybe he had some twisted affection for girls, Kat rejected his advances, and he freaked out and killed her. He could have easily staged the whole thing to look like a stranger broke in to ensure no one pointed the finger at him. It would explain why Kat never screamed."

"It's not an unheard of scenario. Scott and Cody were my primary suspects too, but without a body, we couldn't go anywhere with it. Assuming it was Scott, where would he have taken her if he did it? It'd have to be someplace remote—but not too far away. And not a public place, since that would have drawn attention."

"There were woods surrounding the trailer park where Scott lived with Helen," I pointed out. "What about there?"

"Doubtful. The K9 unit already searched that area and nothing turned up. Plus, those woods around their home were too sparse for a decomposing body to go unnoticed. Plus kids play in there; they would have smelled something. We spread out all over that area with dogs and search teams; had every county and every sheriff's office up and down the coast looking out for a girl matching her description. If it was Scott, he couldn't have gone too far because he was back home in bed before Helen woke up.

Unless there is some private land around there that he would have access to. I remember looking, though, and we couldn't find any property records in his name or his family's in the area."

It was hopeless. There were simply too many variables. It would have to be accessible by vehicle but well hidden from the public. Close to Scott's house. Privately owned land. Most likely a forest, since a large patch of fresh dirt in an open field would have been too obvious a makeshift grave. Considering the acres upon acres of properties that met these criteria, it was a search for a needle in an entire field of haystacks.

"Unless Scott knew someone with a large piece of private property," Tristan said, his voice soft and sad, "The reality, Ari, is that most cases like this don't end well. Most don't get closure. I don't think we're ever going to find Kat or give her family the peace they deserve."

"So you're pretty sure she's dead?" I didn't like the reality, but I couldn't pretend it away when it was staring me in the face.

"Unfortunately that's probably what we're looking at, especially for a girl her age. And in most cases a family member or friend is behind it."

That's when it hit me. Candace's picture of Scott and her uncle.

"Or maybe we can. I think I know where she is, Tristan."

❧❧

Two hours later, the department—armed with an emergency search warrant—scoured the rural property owned by Edward Rhoades, Candace's uncle and Scott's hunting buddy. With forty acres of dense woods, it sounded more daunting than it ended up being. An overgrown dirt road cut through the forest, leading to a cabin that hadn't seen use in years. As the canine unit released the cadaver dogs, I picked my way through some overgrown honeysuckle bushes to a small clearing where I saw something colorful, unnatural, sticking up from the ground. I couldn't quite tell what it was, so I inched closer.

Once through the brush, I realized what it was. A grave. With a babydoll, blue eyes staring blankly ahead, placed purposely like a marker on the mound of black earth. Next to the doll was a bouquet of flowers tied together with pink ribbon, the petals wilted and brown, but very likely a couple months old. Old enough for Scott to have placed them here before his death.

In his secret world he memorialized Kat, left her flowers and adorned her grave with her favorite doll.

"Tristan!" I yelled. "You've got to come see this!"

Seconds later a German shepherd bounded through the bushes behind him, then whined as it pawed at the earth, picking up the scent of a body. I didn't want to watch them unearth Kat's tiny body, or see the remnants of Hello Kitty pajamas found wrapped around the bones. I already knew it was her.

As I numbly stole away, I seethed with hatred for Scott. I almost wanted to thank his killer, because Scott had deserved to die. No, more than that, I hoped Scott had been tortured. It didn't matter that I couldn't ask Scott why; I would never understand it.

The question wasn't what happened to Kat Brannigan, or who killed her and why. The big question marks were: who knew what Scott had done, and why did they wait two years to kill him?

Chapter 29
Ari

On two black metal folding chairs, Helen and Cody Brannigan sat side by side, hands clasped together and fingers intertwined, in a bare-bones conference room as Tristan delivered the news. On the other side of the wall I played with Tempest, occupying her with a coloring book and crayons I'd found in the waiting area near the reception desk. It would be weeks before the medical examiner could identify Kat with certainty, but the clothing, body size, and location were convincing enough to suggest it was their missing daughter. After Tristan handled the tears and questions, I'd be following up with them to get Kat's dental records to help verify the body's identity, a task I dreaded.

I'd discovered that the bulk of private investigation revolved around the tedium of legwork, with an occasional adrenalin rush when you finally got to connect all the dots. That's how I got my rocks off. Then there was the human factor, the painfully emotional realization that you're dealing with people's lives and losses, not just names, numbers, and statistics. I pretty much sucked at that part.

A wail cut through the conversation. I stood up, telling Tempest to stay put while I peered through the rectangular glass window that looked into the door of the conference room. I saw a woman whose hope had been shattered. The same hope had haunted and taunted me for years: that I would one day get my family back, that what was lost would be found. It had taken a decade for me to realize hope was a cruel farce.

The day of my rude awakening hadn't faded over time. That dark night remained an eidetic image in my mind— the hard and heavy weight crushing my chest, filling my entire being with a dull, throbbing ache. I had thought I was dying at the time. Wasn't I too young for a heart attack? I nearly begged my foster home roommate to call 9-1-1, until I realized I wouldn't mind dying right then and there. As a forlorn teenager with no promising future, death felt preferable to me than the perpetual self-hate and loneliness I suffered.

But I didn't die. Instead I received something far worse than death. A realization that my family was never coming back for me, they didn't give a crap about me, I was utterly alone. Forever.

Helen's face crumpled into that same sadness I felt all those years ago. The finality of Kat's death like a knife in the gut. Closure wasn't always a relief. Sometimes benign false hope was better.

I stepped away from the window, unable to stomach watching Helen's pain on display as her face fell into her hands, her palms soaked in her tears, Cody's arm rubbing comforting circles on her back. I wondered if the tragedy would bring them back together. Sometimes things worked out that way.

I needed a drink. Preferably something harder than water, but that would do for now. As I walked to the water cooler, the conference room door opened, and Tristan stepped out. Our eyes met, and he headed straight for me.

"Hey, how are they taking the news?" I asked.

"Helen's a mess, but she seemed relieved that Kat isn't

suffering anymore." Then Tristan leaned in conspiratorially. "Though I think Cody knows more than he's saying."

"What makes you think that?"

"He wasn't surprised, or emotional. I mean, yeah, he's a guy and he might have come to terms with the likelihood of his daughter's death for a while now, but his reaction isn't ... normal. This was his favorite child. They had a special bond. I would expect at least anger—any kind of emotion. I've done this enough times—too many—that I sense when something is off. Especially when it's a parent losing a child."

"You think he's behind it?"

He shrugged. Sighed wearily, as if burdened by the weight of truth. "What do I think? I think he already knew Scott did it and killed him. They're sweeping the cabin for DNA and fingerprints, so hopefully if Cody was there something will turn up."

"What about Jackson Jones? That would mean it's not the same killer ... right?"

"I dunno. I need to look into it more. I, meaning *me*. Not you. Got it?"

"You know I'm gonna do what I'm gonna do, right? I didn't come this far just to sit on the sidelines watching everyone else."

"Okay, I agree," he said, pulling me into a hug. "You earned it. You found Kat, gave her family peace of mind. Maybe I've been a little too hard on you. Just ... promise me you'll stay out of trouble. I'm only asking because I care about you, and I'm scared to death something might ... happen to you."

"Is it because you luuuurve me?" I teased, playfully poking his ribs.

"Lurve is an awfully strong word, but maybe something like that." He briskly kissed me on the forehead and turned back toward the conference room.

"My, my, detective!" With my hand I feigned waving a fan at my face, using my best *Gone with the Wind* Southern drawl. "In the office of all places? You naughty boy!"

Glancing back as he walked away, he pointed his finger at me. "Ari, I mean it. Don't do anything crazy!"

Then the lyrics of an oldie but a goodie by Harold Melvin & the Blue Note started dancing through my brain, and made their way to my lips. "If you don't know me by now," I crooned off-key, until Tristan's stink-eye made me shut the hell up.

Chapter 30

Ari

Two months ago ...

Most days Cody Brannigan liked his job. It offered the distraction he needed from the pain that had chewed at his heart day after day for the past twenty-one months and fourteen days. He liked fixing the employees' computers when a hard drive crashed, or installing new software when an update came through. The pay wasn't great—the Department of Social Services always got the leftovers from the government's budget, and every year it seemed like they made more cuts—but the benefits and paid time off made up for it.

Cody long ago lost faith that the government—like many cynical Americans, he used the term as a pejorative for what he saw as an unchecked leviathan feeding on its own excesses—attached any importance to the growing needs of the poor, the underprivileged, the marginalized. Unwed single mothers. Children born into poverty. Foster children. And the list grew on and on of those who applied for their services. While the numbers of the needy grew, the dollars allotted them shrunk. A vicious cycle that siphoned any chance of betterment for a hopeless minority of Americans.

Sitting at his desk, the past hour empty and quiet, he wondered why he hadn't taken the day off. While it'd been weeks since Scott Guffrey was found dead, the cops were still buzzing around, this morning pulling Cody in for questioning ... again. Unusual circumstances in that neighborhood for a man to be stabbed to death in his own living room. Cody chided himself; he should have called in sick, distanced himself from the office gossip about him as he walked in late after his police *interview*—hell, it was an *interrogation*, pure and simple. He had grown weary of the whole thing, from the media circus that still permeated every news outlet, Facebook page, office, and street corner. The perpetual drama was draining, a raw reminder of what happened to Kat.

His eyes shone with fresh tears, the taste of salt filling his mouth. He needed a phone call to answer, an email to reply to, a computer to fix. Anything to empty his crowded thoughts. That was his favorite part of working here—always something to do. Except for today, when he really needed it. The mundanity of the nine-to-five grind gave him something to look forward to each morning. Anything was better than the empty space in his bed where Kat used to curl up next to him in the dead of night; in the morning he'd turn over to find her eyes closed but lips grinning. While she pretended to be asleep, he'd pretend not to see her as he rolled over on her until she'd puddle into a fit of giggles and squeals. These were the fondest memories, the daily ones that he missed so much. The ones that had become part of his everyday existence. These moments made him who he was.

Who was he without her? For the past twenty-one months and fourteen days he had become no one. An automaton that was good at his job. But it was no kind of life, and he didn't try to fool himself otherwise.

He had survived his own child. He couldn't move on, no matter how hard he tried. The newest victim was Tempest, the *other daughter,* like she was a shadow of what he lost, an apparition of Kat, there but not really. His weekend visits with Tempest hadn't been enough to fill the void. He'd never connected with her like he did Kat, not in the fun way. Kat was his firstborn, a daddy's girl who hung on his every word, lived to please him with her silly jokes, goofy expressions, and playful antics. A jokester, like him. An out-and-out tomboy. Yet the depth of her compassion, her understanding of the world, revealed itself when she would wrap her small arms around his neck, her bright eyes evoking an understanding of the harsh realities of life as she'd remind him, "Daddy, someday life will get better."

Tempest, her polar opposite, was coolly impassive, much like her mother. A bookworm, but she also had a temper like her mom's. So much so, in fact, that sometimes he could barely tolerate her when she got mouthy.

The ring of his desk phone startled him. It was Jackson Jones, a longtime colleague and friend, the one who actually found him the job here at the Department of Social Services.

"Hey, man. Computer crashed again. Can you take a look?"

"Sure, I'll be right there."

Another computer frozen, another unsuccessful reboot. God only knows what Jackson had done to his computer this time with all his online gaming and internet browsing that they were "prohibited" from doing.

Five minutes later Cody sent Jackson to the break room so he could tinker with the computer. Five more minutes later and he'd figured out why Jackson's computer kept crashing. The idiot had forgotten to wipe his browsing history ... and evidence of all the viruses he'd pretty much invited from downloading porn.

As Cody went about emptying the cache, one of the

links looked odd to him. He clicked on it and was confronted with a horrifying picture of a nude little girl. Maybe five or six. Kat's age when she was taken. Tempest's age now. His stomach lurched. His vision swam.

His finger reflexively closed the browser as he felt his head fog, the earth shift and slip. This had to be a mistake. Jackson certainly couldn't ... wouldn't ... Not children. Not his friend. A man he golfed with, played poker with, for crying out loud.

When Jackson returned, a shallow pool of anger within Cody rose, his body shaking with white-hot anger. Jackson's face registered shame in his beady, wide eyes and creased forehead.

"What is this crap on your computer, Jackson? Are you looking at kiddie porn?" His finger jabbed Jackson's chest mercilessly. "And don't lie, because I saw what I saw."

Jackson's lips moved but his words were stuck somewhere in his throat. It was all the affirmation Cody needed.

"I can't believe this. I should turn you in to the cops, man. You're sick!" Several heads popped up from their cubicles around the room.

"Shhh!" Jackson begged. "Please don't tell anyone. Melanie will kill me."

"Oh, you think Melanie will kill you? Wait until your fellow inmates get a hold of you."

"It's not what you think. I was only just looking once."

"Once—like that's any better? The fact that you're looking at it at all is messed up! I don't even know what to say." Clenching his fists, he inhaled, exhaled, inhaled, exhaled. It was a meditative trick his psychiatrist had taught him to get through the panic attacks shortly after Kat went missing. Back when the anxiety first started. It was the same psychiatrist Jackson had recommended.

"We've been friends forever, Cody. I'm already getting help. Please give me a chance. As a friend."

"Friend? I don't even know you anymore." Clench, release. Clench, release.

"I swear, it's not as bad as it looks. I'm getting better—seeing a professional."

The thought struck Cody that Jackson had been seeing his therapist for this exact problem ... for years. This wasn't a one-time deal, was it?

"You make me sick, Jackson. I can't even look at you." Cody turned away, closing his eyes against the roiling in his stomach.

"Please, man, don't tell anyone."

"I can't promise that. And Helen needs to know, because I don't want you anywhere near Tempest. She needs to know not to bring Tempest to your place when she's visiting Melanie. Who she tells, well, that's up to her."

They both knew Helen Brannigan wasn't exactly famous for keeping her mouth shut.

Chapter 31
Ari

Helen and Cody looked perfectly miserable across the table from me. Tristan had suggested I join them in the conference room, creating as casual an environment as possible to get Cody's guard down. If ever there was a time for him to slip up, now would be it, while emotions were running high and defenses dropped. Only hours ago we'd found Kat's badly decomposed body. Only hours ago the truth—well, part of it, anyway—came out. The uncertainty was over. As far as the state was concerned, Kathryn Juliet Brannigan was officially deceased.

Tristan's hunch was that Cody killed Scott to retaliate for Kat's death. The most logical conclusion was usually the right one. It made the most sense, except that it still left Jackson Jones out of the equation. Our objective: pin Cody into a corner. Find out what he was hiding. The only problem with corners was that the only way out was with a fight. And based on his assault record, Cody looked like he'd had a lot of practice fighting.

"I—I don't even know what to say," I began. "I know this isn't the outcome you had hoped for." I studiously avoided the old cop standby "I'm sorry for your loss," which had been robbed of its sincerity by overuse. A cheap condolence couldn't encompass the real heartbreak I felt for both of them.

The box of tissues at Helen's elbow was nearly half empty now, with the other half balled up in a fluffy white mountain on the table, spilling onto the stained berber carpet.

"I just don't know who would have done this to Kat and why. I really don't understand it." Helen shook her head, dabbing at the tears staining her cheeks.

"Things like this ... the horrors that happen ... I don't think we can ever understand them, Helen." I rested my hand gently on hers. "We think it might have been Scott Guffrey, your ex-fiancé."

"But why? There has to be a why," Helen persisted. "Scott adored her. Why would he kill her in cold blood?"

"Helen ... did you ever notice any ... inappropriate touching?"

"Are you kidding me? Do you really think I'd let him stick around if I did?" Her faced burned a livid red; her cheeks puffed. "If I ever saw anyone act inappropriate with one of my girls, I promise you his death would be far worse than what Scott experienced."

"I'm sorry, but I had to ask."

Hollywood made it look easy, but interrogation was a helluva lot harder than it looked. Outsmarting someone, catching them in a lie, exposing inconsistencies—it wasn't easy. I could now understand why cops had forty-eight hours to detain someone ... because at this rate, it'd take that long to drag anything of use from this couple.

A squeeze on my knee gave me the encouragement I needed. I glanced over at Tristan, who nodded almost unperceptively to urge me to keep going. Don't give up. Practice makes perfect. All those useless mantras you shrug off until you realize just how much you need one.

I needed another angle. An angle that tied them to the Southern Slicer, a sensational nickname coined by the media for the killer shortly after my father's attack. Still in a coma, there had been no progress and his diagnosis remained grim. How our "sleepy little town"—aren't all towns called sleepy until something wicked comes this way?—had become the home of such evil was frightening. Sex trafficking. Child murder. Three stabbings in as many months. This notoriety drew a lot of attention in idyllic Bible-belt towns like Durham.

The police captain had kept as many details as possible out of the hands of reporters, like the exact location where Kat was found. You never wanted to show your hand when trying to smoke out a killer.

Once the media got wind of Scott's ties to Kat's murder, the Southern Slicer moniker popped up all over the news and couldn't be squashed, no matter how much the police department pushed back. When word of a serial killer on the loose spread like a California wildfire, citywide panic was always a "breaking news" report away. Our only hope of curbing the flames was to find him … and soon. The only way to do that was to learn as much about Cody Brannigan as I could.

"I'm assuming you'll be taking bereavement leave from work?" I intimated. "Where did you say you work again?"

"Department of Social Services," Cody answered. "And yeah, it's best I spend some time with Helen and Tempest for a while. Get my head together."

And yet his head seemed perfectly clear to me. Too clear.

"Social Services, huh?" Tristan piped up. "The offices on North Duke Street?"

"Yep, that's the one."

"Do you know a man by the name of Jackson Jones? He worked there too—same building, I think."

"Why? Do you think he had something to do with Kat's death?" Helen interjected.

"We're exploring that possibility. Do you know him?"

"Yeah, we've been friends for years. Well, I'm friends with his wife, Melanie. Jackson died last month—killed in his car right outside his house. They think it was the Southern Slicer. But I guess you know all about the case."

Tristan nodded.

"Well, the bastard got what he deserved, if you ask me."

"Jackson, you mean. How so?" Tristan asked.

"I found out he was looking at child porn. As a mother, well, I think child predators should be strung up by their balls." Helen glanced over at Cody. "Tell them. The man was a pervert. Cody worked with Jackson, found porn on his computer. Cody told me, I told Melanie."

I had noticed that Cody was unusually quiet during our chat. But this little tidbit of information was enlightening. Case-altering. Two victims, both connected to Cody, both targeting children.

"Cody, care to elaborate?"

Tristan's jaw clenched and his eyes sparked. We were both thinking the same thing.

"That's really all there is to it. I was fixing his computer, found a child porn site, told him to stop or I'd turn him in."

"You realize what he was doing is highly illegal, right? Why didn't you turn him in to the police? You have daughters, Cody. How could you overlook that?" Tristan pushed.

"Look, we'd been friends forever. I didn't want to jump to conclusions. Plus he told me it was a one-time thing and he was getting help."

"Is this why his wife filed for divorce?"

Helen hurled herself back into the conversation, gesticulating excitedly. "Yeah, though I'm surprised she didn't do worse to him. I think she just didn't know what to do. Then he ends up dead shortly after the divorce paperwork is started. I guess justice comes in many forms.”

“Did Scott and Jackson know each other?” I asked.

“Not that I’m aware of. After Cody and I split up, I didn’t associate with Jackson, just Melanie. So there was no reason for Scott and Jackson’s paths to cross, right, Cody?”

“Yup, that’s right.”

And yet everything felt so wrong.

“Well, I just wanted to again tell you how sorry I am about Kat. Along with the autopsy report, the crime scene investigators found evidence that will help us determine the exact circumstances of your daughter’s death.”

“Do you think they’ll be able to figure out what happened … in her final moments?” Helen broke into a sob mid-sentence. “Was she raped? Was she tortured? I don’t want to know, but I feel like I need to.”

Wrapping an arm around Helen, Cody pulled her against him.

“Honey, she wasn’t tortured or raped. Don’t think like that.”

“But how do you know? You can’t possibly know what she went through. If she had to suffer, I should suffer with her! I should feel the horrors she felt. I feel like such a fool. Why didn’t I recognize that the man I almost married—the man who killed my little girl—was a monster? The only reason anyone would have to kill a child was if she fought back when he was trying to—oh, God help me!”

Helen gave vent to an animalistic cry of pain. Her body shuddered in inconsolable grief for her little girl, violated and murdered.

“Helen, she’s at peace now. Everything that happened in that cabin is in the past. Let it go, let our daughter rest in peace."

"What cabin?"

"Scott's hunting cabin."

"Scott didn't have a hunting cabin."

"Cody, we never mentioned the cabin." Cody's eyes grew wide as he looked up at me. "How do you know about that?"

I could feel Tristan watching me with a glow of pride.

Cody's face lost all color. "Scott had a hunting cabin, I think. At least that's what he told me. I don't know for sure." He lifted both palms up in a gesture of surrender.

"Can you tell me what he's talking about?" Helen directed the question to me.

"Cody's referring to the cabin where Kat was murdered, which belonged to Scott's ex-girlfriend's uncle," I explained. "How he knows this confidential information, that's a good question." Then I turned to Cody.

"I ... I ... must of heard it somewhere," he stammered.

"If you have something to admit, now's the time. Our CSIs managed to pull some prints and DNA from the cabin. We're pretty sure it's the killer's DNA, which we expect will confirm it was Scott." A little cocktail of exaggerations never hurt anyone, since I had no idea if the CSIs found anything at all. "So Scott never mentioned this place to you, Helen? You two were engaged, after all."

"No, I never even knew he had a relationship with Candace's family. He'd never told me about that."

"Are you both sure you know nothing?" Tristan jumped in, his sharp gaze passing from one face to the other. "Now's the time to come clean. Otherwise, if we discover you withheld vital information, well, it won't look good for you."

Helen shook her head. "No, this is news to me."

"And yet you knew about the cabin, Cody?" I stared at him, maintaining my poker face as best I could, though we both knew I had a royal flush.

"Why am I just hearing about this now?" Helen shrieked. "What—you and Scott were all palsy-walsy, and you never told me about it? What else don't I know?"

"What's the big deal? We made small talk, got along—for *your* sake and for the girls."

"Were you ever there, Cody?" Tristan said. "Because if we find your DNA there, now's the time to tell us before it looks suspicious."

"Okay, okay, I went hunting there with Scott once or twice."

"Which was it—once or twice?" Helen pounced.

Cody's neck flushed as he tripped over his words. I wondered if Helen wanted a new career, because she was a damn good interrogator. A bloodhound with a nose for lies.

"Once, it was only once. Geez, Helen, calm down. You're making something out of nothing."

"Do you remember when you were there?" It didn't take a body language expert to figure out he was lying. The trembling hands, the blinking, the quiver in his voice said it all.

"I dunno, it was a long time ago. Right before Kat went missing, I think."

I didn't know if we'd find evidence that put Cody there the night of Kat's death, but he slipped up, and that was enough to justify a much deeper look. He confessed to being in that cabin, which meant he was at the scene of Kat's murder. His demons were running loose, and I was determined to catch them.

Chapter 32

Two months ago …

Cody Brannigan burst through the front door of his ex-wife's trailer in a whirlwind of frantic footsteps. In the middle of the living room Scott Guffrey's oldest son, Kevin, stood with a Wii remote in his hands playing Ping-Pong against Tempest, who jumped up and down next to him.

"Tempest, where's your mother?" he demanded in the brusque tone he reserved exclusively for his other daughter—the one who wasn't Kat. Both video combatants were oblivious to him.

"Ha! Beat you again!" Tempest cheered while Kevin groaned at another loss to a six-year-old.

"No fair. You're hustling me, Tempest! We only get fighter pilot video games in the Air Force, so I can't practice Ping-Pong like you do."

"Too bad, so sad." Tempest rolled her fists beneath her eyes in a mock baby cry, sticking her tongue out in teasing petulance. "Hey, what's *hustling* mean anyway?"

"Go ask your mom."

"Yeah, where the hell *is* Helen?" Cody demanded hotly. Kevin nodded his head almost imperceptibly in the direction of the bedroom. Cody found her there, folding laundry.

"What's that kid doing here?" he sneered.

"You mean Kevin? He has a name, *Cody*."

"Fine, what's *Kevin* doing here? His father is gone. He has no reason to be here."

Helen sighed extravagantly. "No, his father is *dead*. Kevin got bereavement leave to come to Scott's funeral—which you should have done too—and stopped by to say hi to Tempest. Just because he lost his father doesn't mean he lost us as his family. The poor kid is stuck in Florida away from his family while everything back home falls apart. So how about you cut him some slack?"

"Sorry, it just caught me off guard seeing him here."

"Well, keep your voice down. I don't want him hearing you. You know how paper thin these walls are."

"Sorry."

As Helen emptied the last of the laundry basket, she bustled out of the bedroom and into the living room, grabbing rumpled clothing from the sofa, floor, and entryway.

"Tempest!" But Tempest was too busy lording another win over Kevin to hear her mother. "Clean up after yourself. There's no reason you should be undressing yourself all over the house. My goodness ..."

With a distracted "mmkay," Tempest resumed her Ping-Pong mastery while Helen continued collecting dirty clothes.

"So what brings you storming into my home uninvited?" Helen asked while Cody trailed puppyishly behind her as she weaved in and out each room.

"Jackson. I found child porn on his computer today."

Helen stopped in her tracks, wide-eyed and mouth gaping in a silent gasp. "What? Are you serious?"

"Dead serious. And he'll be a dead man if he ever goes near Tempest. I wanted to warn you in person so that you don't let that perv anywhere near our daughter."

"Does Melanie know?"

"No, no one does ... yet. But in case Melanie wants to

hang out and see you and Tempest, it can't be at their house if he's there. Okay?"

"Of course. You know I have to tell Melanie, right? Though how I'm going to break this to her ... I don't even know what to say. How do you tell a friend she has no idea who her husband is ... that she's married to a monster?"

He often wondered this exact question. How could he ever confess to Helen what he'd done? She had no idea who she had been married to, what he was capable of. And yet did any married couple really ever know the ones they committed their souls to? They vowed "for better or worse," but no one wanted to know the "worse" part. Didn't everyone have secrets, some more sinister than others?

"I don't care if or how you say it to Melanie, as long as he doesn't go near our daughter."

Helen rolled her neck, rubbing the taut tendon along her shoulder. "This is seriously too much. First Scott getting murdered. Now having to tell my best friend that her husband is a pedophile. I can't take much more, Cody. Ever since Kat ..." her voice trailed off. She'd never been able to state the obvious, that Kat had been killed. Instead she used hopeful terms like *disappeared* or *left,* as if Kat had made the choice to pack her bags and hit the road. "I'm fragile now. I've seen too much ugliness."

Sliding up behind the only woman he had ever truly loved, he rested his hands on her shoulders, massaging them like he'd done a million times before, back when they were together. He missed her so much sometimes.

"Honey"—the endearment slipped out from habit—"it's not your problem to deal with. You've got enough on your plate."

"I know, but this is Melanie we're talking about, my friend since forever, not some acquaintance. And Jackson hasn't been well. Apparently he's already on anti-depressants. It's gonna kill him if she leaves him."

"Then the sicko will get what he deserves."

"I thought he was your friend."

Cody laughed contemptuously. "No one who looks at child porn is my friend. Would you stay friends with a child molester?" Helen shook her head slowly and emphatically. "But hey, I gotta run. I just wanted to tell you so you knew to keep a safe distance."

As Cody left, Helen wondered if any distance was safe enough.

Chapter 33
Ari

It'd been eight long hours and I was already burning out. I listened from behind the one-way conference room glass as Tristan grilled Cody Brannigan about why forensics had found his fingerprints at the cabin, why his blood DNA was discovered on the Hello Kitty shirt Kat was wearing when she was killed, what he knew about what happened to his daughter that night.

Eight hours. A whole shift for the average working stiff. A cop's day was almost always longer. This day looked to be endless.

All at once Cody stopped idly picking at the scab on his elbow. His face went slack.

The bastard was about to crack.

Dropping his head into his hands, he began to cry, a howl that shook his body and penetrated the walls. Finally the breakdown that Tristan searched for. Finally the confession that would explain what exactly happened to Kat in her last moments.

"What happened that night?" Tristan's demand caused the glass to tremble. "Based on what we've found, you're looking at murder charges."

"Murder charges?"

Cody jolted upright, panic blazing in eyes red from crying.

"For Scott Guffrey."

"Hey, I had nothing to do with Scott's death."

"And Jackson Jones."

"What? No, you've got it all wrong."

"Then set me straight, Cody. Now's the time to come clean with everything, and I mean *everything*, and maybe we can help you stay out of jail."

Cody slumped forward, resting his hand on his forehead while his eyes blankly examined a metal folding table that held no answers. His face matched the gray of the walls. I imagined his thoughts trickling through this head like a babbling brook, rushing over rocks along a rough-hewn course. There was no damming the path now. Cody was floundering in the riptide and the only way out was the truth.

Lifting his head slowly to meet Tristan's eyes, anguished tears coursed down his cheeks. I felt sorry for the guy. Sort of.

"It was an accident, I swear. It all started when Helen threatened to take full custody ..." Cody began. His words weighed heavy like a falling ax. "She was marrying Scott and wanted to have the girls full-time. Said it was a more stable environment. Then she tells me they'll be moving. I'd only see Kat maybe once a month. Once a month!" He glared challengingly at Tristan. "Detective, do you have a daughter?"

"No, I don't," Tristan answered.

"So you wouldn't understand. But when the only person you care about in the world—your daughter—is being taken away from you, you have to fight back. Fight dirty. Do whatever it takes to save what you have."

"You keep mentioning Kat, but what about Tempest?"

Cody made an ugly guttural sound. "I doubt Tempest is biologically mine. I don't have a DNA test or anything to prove one way or another, but Helen cheated on me right before she got pregnant with Tempest. And the kid looks nothing like me and we have nothing in common ... so, you do the math."

"Then why do you stick around?"

"I love Tempest, don't get me wrong, but it was harder with her because she's a reminder of what Helen did. I mean, sure, I play the role of dad because I'm all Tempest knows, but Kat was my flesh and blood. My firstborn. It's just ... special when it's your blood. A unique connection."

"You said you fought back. How?" I watched admiringly as my boyfriend worked, masterfully massaging the facts out of Cody. Tristan was picking at his words, little pinpricks that would let the truth shine through. I had so much to learn.

"When I found out they were moving, I approached Scott. I knew a guy who knew a guy willing to help for the right price, and I was able to convince Scott it was the right thing to do ... He's a father, so he understood."

"What was the right thing to do?"

"Fake Kat's abduction, then I'd run off with her."

Two years ago ...

The plan sounded simple enough. But nothing was ever as simple as saying the words. Words were easy. Action was a whole 'nother ballgame. Predictable results even harder yet.

The clock on Cody's truck dashboard said he was early, but Scott Guffrey's rusted-out blue Ford and Norman Bledsoe's white Chevy were already parked in the muddy open area beside the porch. Stepping out of his truck, he heard the screams of a little girl—*his* little girl— and sprinted to the cabin's front porch, flinging the door open to see Scott and Norman in a deadly standoff.

Norman waving a gun, Scott attempting to talk him down from whatever stupidity his high had him rambling about—a seething chaos that could only end badly. Deadly. Cody hadn't thought this part through when he agreed to do business with a drug addict.

"Daddy!" Kat screamed from one side of the small, musty room. She pushed past Scott's legs, until his grip on her shoulder stopped her.

"Don't you move," Norman demanded from the other side of the room, his arm pivoting back and forth between Scott and Cody. A crumbling stone fireplace rose up into the ceiling behind him, the kitchen on the other side of that. The space was so cramped that Cody felt the air stir as they all breathed harder. A gun quivered in one hand while the other habitually rubbed at his left eye. He was flying high, strung out like the rainbow tail of Kat's princess kite. His bony limbs jumped and jolted as if electric surges pulsed through him.

"Norm, what the hell, man? Put the gun down."

"Change of plans." Norman began to pace, one spindly arm rotating the gun from Kat to Cody, Cody to Kat, Kat to Scott. "Your friend here thinks he can just walk away. But she's worth a lot more if I sell her. Already got an interested buyer, George Battan. Pays real good, too. So unfortunately for you, I'm taking her with me."

"I'll pay you whatever you want if you just put the gun down," Cody said, forcing a calm he didn't feel.

"You can't afford my price."

While Kat wailed against Scott's side, Cody plotted his next step. He should have known not to trust Norman to follow through. A few days—that was all he had needed, just to establish an alibi and appear blameless. Then he'd pretend to go in search of Kat, meanwhile taking her to start a new life far away from this dump they'd called home for too long.

So the plan wasn't foolproof. No one had ever accused him of having common sense, but it had sounded like it could work. With enough monetary incentive, anything could work. Scott would pretend to abduct her. Norman would keep her entertained for a few days while the police searched for her, then when the hunt died down, he'd come up with some reason to head for the hills. His only problem was trusting a drug addict to do his part. Stupidly, he hadn't anticipated greed coming into play.

"Look, I'll find a way to come up with whatever your price is. Don't do this to an innocent kid, Norm. Be a man of your word."

Norman laughed, revealing the toll years of meth use had exacted on his teeth. "You think my word's worth shit? Money talks, Cody, and Battan's talking loud."

"Oh come on!" Scott was clearly done with negotiations as he pushed Kat behind him and lunged at Norman. "Think about what you're doing, dude. Cody just wants to be with his daughter. That's all. We all agreed. This ain't right, man."

Norman threw up his palm. "Stop right there!"

All Cody could think about was disarming him before he ended up killing someone. Glancing at Scott, their eyes met in an unspoken agreement to throw together a Plan B. One that involved taking Norm out by any means necessary.

"Let's sit down and talk this through. I'm sure we can come up with something that'll work for everyone," Cody said in a soothing voice he reserved for the kids.

While he distracted Norman with careful steps toward him, Scott lunged at him from the other side, throwing his arms around Norman, both of them grappling over the gun. While Scott managed a jab to Norm's chin, Norm smacked the barrel of the gun against Scott's temple. The searing pain nearly blinded him, hiding his target in the shadows of his vision, so he threw blind punches until he connected with flesh. Pulling Scott into a fierce hug, Norm immobilized them both, so Scott kicked what felt like Norm's shin again and again. Together they fell to the floor, yelping, arms whaling, bones crunching, fingers grabbing, legs searching for purchase on the filthy floor. All while Kat stood stock-still, crying in the middle of the room.

Cody jumped in to pull them apart and find the gun, receiving a blow that broke his nose. Blood trickled down his lip, but adrenaline fueled him past the pain and the metallic taste oozing down his throat. Again he leapt into the fray. He got the breath knocked out of him, but only for a second. Then he was back in it. Amid the grunting and cussing and flailing limbs, a shot rang out.

Everyone stopped. A momentary lull. Hands searched their own bodies for injuries.

Then Kat crumpled to the floor.

Cody ran to her, pulling her against his chest. Blood blossomed on her shirt, whether from the droplets dripping from his nose or the wound he couldn't find, he wasn't sure. Scanning her body for the hole, he cried out for help.

But no help would ever be enough.

As Cody's guilt gushed out in tears and contrition, I realized no jail sentence could punish him as much as he had been punishing himself for the past two years. Helen assured him she'd stand by him while they got through this, she understood why he did what he did, would forgive him eventually. Not now, for the revelation of his role in Kat's death was still too fresh, but time would heal these wounds, she told him. Time would help her forgive. These promises she offered him as a gift. Despite her benevolence, we all knew Cody was undeserving of such kindness. He had tried to kidnap his own daughter and as a result got her killed.

By the time Tristan got Cody's written testimony, my cell phone buzzed on silent mode for the umpteenth time. Checking my missed calls, I saw I had a voicemail message and clicked to listen:

"Ari, something's happened. I need you to come home as soon as you get this."

I had missed the call from Tina about an hour ago while watching Cody's confession unravel. Ever since the second threat letter I had received, I had insisted that she stay at my apartment with me until the killer was caught. It took several arguments to finally get her to agree, but only after I offered her my bedroom. Her safety was worth me sleeping on the sofa. After my four callbacks all went straight to voicemail, I clocked out and broke every speed limit on my way home.

When I arrived at my apartment, I opened the unlocked door to find Tina lying unconscious on the living room floor, a letter fluttering peacefully at her side as a blast of air-conditioning lifted its corners. Kneeling down next to her, she almost looked like she was sleeping. No blood anywhere. No evidence of a stab wound.

Thank God.

I instinctively reached down and pressed my fingertips to Tina's neck, checking for a pulse. Alive. Picking up Tina's limp body, I cradled her in her arms, talking her back to wakefulness like I was inviting a child to join me in a tea party.

"Tina, honey, you're okay. I need you to wake up now. Come on, wakey wakey."

I gave Tina's cheeks a couple of short, sharp slaps.

Finally her eyelids fluttered open against the harsh afternoon sunlight streaming in through the sliding glass door.

"What happened?" Tina asked, reaching for the back of her head.

"I was hoping you could tell me."

When Tina withdrew her hand, I looked at it. No blood. That was a good sign. I picked up the letter and began to piece together the puzzle of what happened:

YOU HAVE HAD ENOUGH WARNINGS. IT'S D-DAY FOR YOU. YOU MUST STOP LOOKING FOR ANSWERS. THE ENEMY MUST BE PUNISHED. DO NOT FIGHT THEIR BATTLE OR YOU WILL SUFFER. THE WAR HAS ONLY BEGUN. YOU'D MAKE A HELLUVA JANE WAYNE, NOW EMBRACE THE SUCK.

It was another cryptic message apparently from the Southern Slicer ... who wasn't Cody, because right now Cody was at the precinct with Tristan. Whoever it was, he was still out there. And until he was caught, I wasn't safe, Tina wasn't safe, my father wasn't safe, Giana wasn't safe. What if he went for Giana next? The threat lingered in the dead air between us.

"Do you remember anything?" I asked Tina.

Tina cupped her forehead, squinting in pain. I imagined she was probably experiencing the mother of all migraines.

"I can't think ... I'm not sure. I remember getting out of the shower and getting dressed. Then coming into the living room to watch TV when I saw the letter on the table. I was reading the letter, that's when I called you. After that it's a blur. I think I remember something slamming into the back of my head, then feeling dizzy. I don't recall anything after that ... like when I passed out."

"You didn't see anyone at all? No movements or

shadows?"

"No, I never saw it coming or who did it. I'm sorry, Ari."

I hugged her to my chest like she was my own. "No, don't be sorry, sweetie. You didn't do anything wrong. This maniac just isn't gonna give up."

The persistence. The threats. The restraint. The killer could have taken Tina's life but chose not to. This twisted vigilante apparently knew about Scott Guffrey's involvement in Kat's death, Jackson's porn addiction, and my dad's cover-up in Marla's murder. And yet this person was also misinformed, because Scott hadn't killed Kat in cold blood. And my father only got targeted because of a misleading news report.

It was someone obscure enough to linger on the outskirts of these lives, smart enough to get away with murder, quick and sneaky enough to use a knife, but stupid enough not to do due diligence in their research.

Helen? Jackson's wife Melanie? Neither felt right.

This person was trustworthy enough to bum a ride with Jackson, a smooth enough talker to get access into Scott's house, but sloppy enough not to finish the job with my father.

There was someone I was overlooking. A clue right in my face. Only one person alive had laid eyes on the killer and survived. And that one person was my only chance at stopping the killer before he struck again.

Chapter 34
Ari

Good afternoon, Mrs. E," I greeted my old neighbor when she answered the door in a bright floral muumuu.

I had brought along a variety box of Dunkin' Donuts. One of the flavors was the closest thing to *paczki* I could find, a Polish fruit-filled cake covered in powdered sugar that Mrs. E used to make from scratch. Back in the day Carli and I would haunt her kitchen window like the little sugar zombies that we were, getting fat on the wonderful smell alone.

Standing on her stoop, I opened the lid of the box to tempt her. "An Americanized version of *paczki*!"

Her penciled brows shot up to her hairline. She waved off the donuts with a sneered "Those are garbage." Then her talon-like fingers gripped my wrist with unexpected strength as she pulled me inside. "But beggars can't be choosers."

Rooting through a stack of newspapers, she cried out, "Aha!" when she located two hidden (and reasonably clean) paper plates and placed them at the kitchen table, one for each of us, then picked a donut—a custard-filled one with chocolate icing. I selected the same.

"I wanted to pick your brain again about what you saw the night my dad was attacked. We're close to catching him, but I really need your sharp memory. Think you can help me?"

"I can certainly try," she said, dabbing at a clump of vanilla custard that hung from the corner of her lips.

"Can you remind me again exactly what you saw? This time close your eyes, imagine yourself in that moment. Where were you standing when you saw everything?"

"Standing right there." Mrs. E pointed a crooked shaky finger at her back door that exited from the kitchen. "I was letting Lucy out."

"Close your eyes and visualize it. You're letting the cat out. Now what do you see? What drew your attention?"

"It was dark, but the streetlights cast a glow, enough that I noticed a shadow moving. Only it wasn't a shadow. It was someone dressed in black. And wearing—what do they call it?—oh, yes, a hoodie. I'm pretty sure it was a man. A smallish man."

"How was he walking?"

"Pretty quickly. Almost like a fast march. But the movements were stiff. He carried himself very erect."

"What about the hands?"

"Gloved."

"Can you see his face?"

"Not really well, but the streetlight looked white against his face. Yes, he was definitely white."

We were getting somewhere. Although the pieces slowly dragged together, coalescing from a blur into a crisp picture, Mrs. E had a conviction in her voice, a determination to help solve the puzzle.

"What about the shoes—did you get a look at the type of shoes?"

"Black boots, I think. Not cowboy style. Shorter."

"Anything else you remember?"

"Yes. He was wearing sunglasses, if you can believe it. The oddest thing at that hour." She smiled apologetically.

"My memory's not what it used to be, sweetie, but I hope this helps."

I smiled back and squeezed her veiny hand. "You've been a tremendous help, Mrs. E. I hope my memory's half as good as yours when I'm in my … sunset years."

"Sunset years, my ass! Honey, I'm just plain older than dirt!"

When our laughter finally faded, I said, "Well, I don't know about that, but with your help I wouldn't be surprised if we catch the guy now."

As she glowed with pride, I realized how important it was to remind our elderly friends that we needed them more than ever to make the world a safer place. In fact, our shut-in neighborhood watchers were the eyes and ears of the community.

After chitchat about her latest feline addition to the family, a black and white stray she named Puddin', I hugged and thanked her, then headed across the street to my dad's house. If the killer had been watching me sneak into the house, it was possible he used the same entry point the night of my dad's attack. I rounded the back of the house to the basement window, where the earth appeared undisturbed since the night of my father's attack.

Huddling over a collage of footprints, I could easily make out the imprints of the sole of my Converse tennis shoe, which I'd splurged on after cashing my first police department paycheck. Then a second set of footprints—a couple sizes larger. Deep prints from a work boot or military boot with rugged, multi-directional lugs for maximum traction; I'd seen a similar pattern on the boots worn by EMTs and members of SWAT. I could just make out the word *Vibram* set in an octagon in the middle, so I took a picture with my cell phone. They definitely weren't my dad's Reeboks or my mom's Easy Spirits.

A quick internet search for "Vibram boots" on my phone returned the most interesting result. Common military-issue boots. My mind dashed back to the lingo in the letters. *You'd make a helluva Jane Wayne.* Where had I heard that name before? Of course—Jane Wayne Day, named after the Duke. All branches of the military had them; a day set aside for wives to experience the challenges their husbands faced on a daily basis. I'd read about one such event at Camp Lejeune. Then there were the *I must soldier on* and the *D-day* references.

That's when I knew who was behind it all.

Chapter 35

Three months ago …

I listened to him cry. Beg for forgiveness. Plead for relief from the guilt. Real men didn't cry. Real men didn't beg. Real men didn't plead. No, real men sucked it up and took their licks.

To set the record straight, I wasn't beaten as a child. I didn't come from an abusive home. A little unconventional, sure, and neglectful, but whose home life was all glitz and glamour? Even the rich snobs making headlines from their reality shows had their fair share of misery. They just suffered while wearing Gucci and gold.

My mother used drugs, my dad drank. But both were high functioning, able to keep jobs and raise their kids while enjoying the occasional fix. My "psychological issues," as my high school guidance counselor euphemistically called my acting out, were a volatile mélange of nature *and* nurture. The counselor said my "domineering social behavior" was characteristic of guys of short stature, like me; a Napoleon complex, he called it. He had it all wrong. I always stood up for the bullied kids for one reason: I saw myself as an underdog too, and I hated seeing someone get the crap beat out of them just because they were different.

Mom and Dad never envisioned college for me, although I'd aced my SATS and had always scored in the top percentile on standardized tests. I blew crap like that off; no kid wants to be labeled a brainiac. My parents always pushed me toward the military—the Air Force in particular. According to them, I was a perfect fit with my leadership traits, which even my stick-up-his-ass principal had begrudgingly acknowledged. I was never among the in-crowd—and had no desire to be—but I was popular with the freaks and geeks and pseudo-intellectuals. Hell, I even ran for student body president— on a dare. Some of my fellow outsiders put me up to it. I mounted a half-ass campaign and, to the surprise of absolutely nobody, I lost big. That was cool with me. Those pussies in student government were self-deluded. Thought their shit didn't stink. There's nothing more contemptible than a cardboard authority figure. Except real authority figures. I despise them.

Anyway, the general thinking, at home and at school, was that maybe, just maybe, the Air Force could instill the discipline in me that my parents, teachers, and administrators couldn't. The world was mine for the taking. I could be a fighter pilot. Or an aerospace propulsion technician fixing planes. Or my top choice: explosive ordnance disposal. Defusing bombs. At least when dealing with bombs it would be a quick and painless death. I have to admit, the idea of messing around with bombs kind of gave me an intellectual hard-on. You know, the danger aspect. Getting blown to smithereens and being branded a hero. Buried in a flag-draped coffin. The whole corny shebang held a morbid appeal for me. Look, Mommy and Daddy, I'm Somebody now.

Yeah, but that was just a bunch of childish bravado. Crazy talk. I wasn't in any real hurry to die. And certainly not for a country that marginalized the citizens that needed Uncle Sam to have their back the most. I went into the military thinking the government gave a shit. How wrong I was. As they passed out painkillers like candy to force injured soldiers to press on, they turned us into addicts while war turned us into sociopaths.

I'd never forget how scared shitless I felt as my parents stood behind me, forcing me to enlist. It was an easy way to erase the mistake they'd made when they had me. Get rid of me in a jiffy by making me the government's problem.

Oddly enough, sending me off was the first time they'd made a united front with anything. When it came to parenting, they were divided. When it came to what we ate for dinner, they were divided. When it came to what house we rented, they were divided. But when it came to shipping me off to my death, they snapped together like the mouth of a clam.

As I scribbled my signature across the bottom of the enlistment contract, I felt like I was signing my own death certificate. I had begged my parents to let me live at home, find a job, maybe even try community college out. But no. They wanted me gone … yesterday. Handed me over to die in some godforsaken Middle Eastern country, their firstborn son. My heart broke and my faith shattered with it as I watched them barter my life away. Six years of freedom from me in exchange for my free will. The deal of a lifetime for them, the nightmare from hell for me. I would never forgive them for it.

One person fought for me, and that was Helen, Dad's fiancée and the only one who gave a crap about me. Over spaghetti dinner one night, Helen, Mikey, and her two girls teamed up against my father, begging him to give me a shot at college instead.

"He's smart. Would probably qualify for grants and stuff," Helen had tried to point out.

The answer, as it always was anytime I wanted anything, was no. That was the first, and probably only time they'd seen my dad's inflexible side.

THE DEATH OF LIFE

As I boarded a plane for Texas a couple weeks later, I vowed never to forgive them for stripping the one thing I had that was my own—my voice. But I would speak again very soon, and loudly enough so that the world would hear.

Apparently just because you suck at life doesn't mean you're fit for a uniform. Weeks into basic training my instructors discovered what everybody else already knew: I was far too much of a headstrong individual to be a good little tin soldier. After all, isn't that what the military's all about is—blindly taking orders? I wore my recalcitrance like a medal. I held on for as long as I could, months of being berated and brainwashed until I didn't recognize myself anymore, but in the end, one's nature always takes over. My nature was telling me to get the hell out of Dodge. Though even still today I kept my boots polished and bed pristinely made with hospital corners. Some habits never die.

I hadn't intended to wash out, especially with nowhere to go. AWOL, the military called it when you just up and disappeared. I was sure they were looking for me, but I'd lost any capacity to care about what happened to me. I hadn't told my family—if I could even call them that—until one day I showed up at my dad's house carrying the duffel bag I had been first shipped off with on one shoulder and the weight of failure on my other.

After my military stint had slaughtered all my old dreams, I lost all sense of purpose along the way. Who was I? What did I want in life? I didn't have a clue.

Until now.

I dropped my bag at the foot of the blue living room sofa that felt like sandpaper. I'd suffer through sleeping on it if it meant I didn't have to deal with my mother.

"You can't live with me. Go live with your mom." I could smell the beer on Dad's breath as he got in my personal space, his body swaying slightly.

"You're a real son of a bitch, you know that? Can't even give your son a place to crash for one night after he comes home from serving his country. Fine, I'll go to Mom's. Can you at least give me a lift?"

His eyelids drooped like anvils weighed them down. His body swayed like he was riding waves. I had never seen him this bad—not in all my childhood or adolescence.

"Just get a taxi or somethin'. I'm in no shape to drive."

Making his way to the kitchen, he tripped over the arm of the sofa and fell into the seat. I wondered if this was just alcohol … or was he on something stronger?

"Are you high? What are you taking?"

"None of your business, *Keeeevinnnn.*" I hated the way he slurred my name when he was drunk. "It's just a little something to make me feel better."

"Feel better how?"

"I'm going through some stuff right now. Just leave me alone."

"Dad, what kind of stuff? You can talk to me."

"See, that's the problem, Keeeeev. I can't talk to you. Can't talk to no one. Just go. Goooooo!"

As if expelling that last word took every last bit of energy he had, he fell back against the cushions.

Then he gained a second wind as one eye peeked lazily open. "I see you judging me. You wanna call me a junkie? Go ahead, say it. But what you don't understand is that I'm a story, with lots of pages. I'm laughter, I'm love. I'm ripped open, I'm scabbed over … Those are my insides, Kev. I'm not just what you see when you look at me." He seemed to consider his own words and gave a self-deprecating snort. "I'm a deep sumbitch, ain't I, Kev? God, what a bunch of horseshit."

I knew depression when I saw it. A seductive

mistress. It enticed with whispered suggestions: *it's easier to hide.* What I saw in my father wasn't just depression. It was darker, grittier, harsher. It was guilt. A soldier ambushing him, slaughtering him from the inside out. He was unsalvageable, much like myself.

"It's no wonder Helen split up with you and Mom didn't want you," I grumbled under my breath. I figured his excessive drinking had something to do with Kat's disappearance. My grandmother had told me about it during one of our monthly calls, said Dad had been falling apart ever since. I guess if something happened to Mikey I would have felt the same. While he wasn't my kid, I had almost raised him myself.

I decided to make a sandwich and called for an Uber, watching him sleep, until I heard a sniffle, then a sob. At the kitchenette table I silently sat, observing him as he fumbled for his cell phone in his pocket and misdialed with a wandering finger, then dialed again with a little more deliberation.

I could hear the other end ringing, then a voice that sounded like a voicemail.

"Cody, man, I can't sleep, I can't eat. I'm just ... I'm so sorry about Kat. It's all my fault. I don't know how to fix this. I feel like she's haunting me from the grave. Every night I see her, the bullet tearing through her, and I know I can't take it all back. Please help me. I don't want forgiveness. You can't possibly give that, I know. I don't deserve it. How do I make it stop? The guilt. The ache in my soul. She's dead ... cuz of me. I ... just wanna die with her, man."

As I stood there listening to my father's murder confession of the girl who would have been my little stepsister, I realized there had been no abduction. The search parties, the media frenzy, the suffering, the worry, the depression, the drugs, the alcohol—my dad had caused it all. He had left Helen's life in shambles. He had taken Kat's life. And now he sat in his own soiled misery wanting freedom from the guilt.

I couldn't free his conscience. But I could free him from the chains of this life. Because that's what child-killers deserved.

Chapter 36
Ari

Candace Guffrey?" Tristan asked as we stood side by side on her doorstep. Glancing at me, I saw the recognition in her eyes, then a glint of pissed-offness. She felt betrayed by her fellow woman, and rightly so.

"Yes?"

"I'm Detective Tristan Cox with the Durham Police Department. May I come in for a moment?"

"I'm sorry, but I'm running late for work. Is this important?"

"Ma'am, I think it's best if you get this over with now. I promise to make it as quick and painless as possible."

Huffing in frustration, she stepped aside and let us in, whispering an audible "Liar" as I passed.

Tristan led the way into the living room, where Candace reluctantly trailed him.

"Can your son join us?"

"What's Mikey got to do with anything? He's five."

"Not Mikey. Kevin. I know he's here."

She paused, folded her arms defiantly across her chest. "I'm sorry, but he's in the Air Force down in Florida. So you're wrong. He's not here."

"Ma'am, don't make this worse than it has to be. We just need to ask him a few questions about his dad." I could hear the strained politeness in Tristan's voice.

"Then ask me. I'll answer whatever you need to know."

"Ms. Guffrey, would you prefer we haul him out of here in handcuffs?"

Rolling her eyes, Candace turned to the hallway. "Kevin!" she yelled. "Get out here please."

When a young man appeared around the corner where the kitchen met the living room, my mouth nearly dropped. He was young—far too young to be the Southern Slicer. He stood there silently, his blue eyes darting between Tristan and me, then resting on mine. A corner of his lips lifted in a secret acknowledgement that he recognized me, knew exactly who I was. His blond buzz cut was growing out, sprouting short curls. And there on his feet were Vibram military boots like the ones I'd seen online. Bingo!

"Kevin Guffrey?" Tristan asked, though we both already knew the answer.

"Yes, sir."

"We'd like to speak with you down at the station."

"Yes, sir."

Without another word, Kevin straightened his back and marched through the living room toward the front door, behind Tristan and me. As Tristan opened it to walk Kevin out, an unseen fist smashed against Tristan's cheek, then another punch smacked him in the nose. Throwing his arms up to protect his face, Tristan ducked blindly as Kevin wound up and delivered a haymaker that sent Tristan stumbling backward into me. We both fell on the floor in a heap.

Behind us Candace yelped, "Kevin!"

Managing to throw my weight toward Kevin's legs, I clawed at his ankle, which was close enough to wrap my fingers around. I pulled at his leg, trying to drag him down to the floor. He wildly kicked at me while I squinted against the foot flying at my face, dodging it as best I could. I didn't see the wheel kick coming from the other direction as the steel toe thudded against my temple, temporarily blinding me. For a long moment my world went black. I felt my grip loosening as he pried at my fingers. I heard Tristan grunt as Kevin kicked him viciously in the head while he was still down. As Kevin royally kicked our asses, his mother shrieked in the background.

When I could see straight again, there went Kevin, darting across the front yard and into the street.

"He's getting away!" I screamed, pushing Tristan off of me and jumping up to my feet. My head and tailbone hurt like hell as my legs pumped, but I ignored the splitting pain. I heard footsteps clapping against the pavement behind me and looked over my shoulder to see Tristan joining the chase, blood dripping down his nose and his eye red and split. But Kevin's head start put him nearly a quarter of a mile ahead of us. I lost sight of him when he cut through a neighbor's yard and dashed into a copse of trees.

My lungs burned and legs ached as I tried to keep pace, entering the clearing where I thought I saw him go. Beyond, the trees grew thick. I knew he was long gone. Several beats later Tristan joined my side, bent over and heaving as he caught his breath.

"I can't believe it. We almost had him." I wanted to cry.

"Get used to the chase," Tristan sputtered between gulps of air. "It's part of the job—which is why you shouldn't let yourself get out of shape like me."

Hunched over, he looked up at me with sorrowful eyes. His face was a mangled mess of swollen bruises and gashes.

"What do you expect from ex-military? Yikes, he really did a number on you." Tristan winced when I gently touched his rapidly purpling eye socket.

"We'll have our chance to get back at him," he said. "We just need to figure out where he went."

Where would a boy with no home go? Did he have friends from high school that he could turn to in an emergency? Or had he distanced himself from everyone? Clearly his mother had been harboring him since his return from the military, but I doubted she would give us any information we needed in order to find him. How the heck were we supposed to find a runaway suspect with nowhere to turn?

"How do we do that?" I whined. "He could be anywhere."

Tristan rested his hand on my shoulder. "Hey, don't worry, we'll find him. We'll put out a BOLO, check local shelters, and send a patrolman over to his grandmother Lillian Guffrey's house," Tristan said, jumping into solution autopilot. While all these worries buzzed through my head, my amazing detective boyfriend was already a step ahead of me. I had so much still to learn. "We'll see if she's seen him or knows where he might be. Helen Brannigan's place too. They had a good relationship; he might feel safe turning to her. And we'll put an alert out on social networks and the media to get his picture everywhere. We've put a face to our suspected killer now. Don't worry. He won't get far."

"You're good, you." I kissed his cheek, the only spot that hadn't been beat to a pulp.

"I know." But his humble grin told me my validation certainly wouldn't hurt.

Several hours later we were still empty-handed. With officers on the lookout at Candace's place, he hadn't returned. Kevin hadn't stopped by Helen's either, though her sincere concern for him was evident in her wet eyes as we told her why we were searching for him. "He was like a son to me," she had said. "I can't believe he'd do something like this."

The shock of Kevin's secret other life seemed contagious. Poor Lillian Guffrey, hairdresser extraordinaire, had a breakdown when we showed up at her doorstep. Her first thought was that Kevin had died in combat—clearly she wasn't aware that the local police weren't the ones to deliver such news. Her second thought was that Kevin couldn't possibly be behind Scott's death, because he was "such a good boy. Such a sweet, smart, well-behaved young man." We had it all wrong, according to Lillian, but she suggested we check Scott's old house to see if it had been rented out yet.

"If there was anyone Kevin would want to turn to right now, it'd be his father," she added. "Sadly, Kevin never had any real friends but his dad. While they had their fair share of differences, Kevin adored Scott. Looked up to him, wanted to be like him. I think he'd want to be close to him in any way he could."

But Scott's place had been leased last month, the new tenants already moved in and unpacked. I found it peculiar that Lillian felt so strongly about the bond between Scott and Kevin. If that was true, why would Kevin have murdered his own father? And that's when a tiny thought began to coagulate.

I had a hunch of where to find a boy who felt desperate, remorseful, and scared, a boy who just needed someone to talk to who wouldn't talk back.

The graveyard was small and tidy, neatly trimmed

aisles between the gravestones, May flowers popping up in a colorful array throughout the grounds. Blue cornflowers, purple delphinium, orange and red gerber daisies grew wild, accompanied by carefully laid bouquets of pink peonies and fuscia stargazer lilies. For a place where the dead dwelled and haunts hung in the tense air, it was quite beautiful. It reminded me of Carli.

I had spotted Kevin across a large expanse of tombstones, sitting on the grass with his chin resting on his knees. I didn't see a killer. I saw a sad, frightened, and confused boy who needed somebody to talk to. I crept up to him, not wanting to alarm him or set him off running again.

"I know what you're going through," I whispered behind him.

He pivoted toward me and scrambled backward, his eyes wide with alarm. His hand reached into his pocket, whipping out a Swiss Army knife. Retracting the blade, he held it aimed at me. "Don't make me kick your ass again. I'm not into beating up chicks."

"I'm just here to talk," I said, palms up in surrender.

"I don't want to talk. I want to be left alone."

"You know I can't do that. By now you have the military police and the entire Durham Police Department looking for you. It's over."

"No, not until I say it's over." The beads of sweat on his forehead and tremble of his hand told me otherwise.

"You have to be tired of running and hiding, aren't you?"

"And go to prison for life? I don't think so." He lunged a step back, knife still poised.

"Prison can't be much worse than what I went through as a kid."

His head tilted. "Like what?"

"Like when my sister was murdered and my parents

blamed me, tossed me into the foster system—group homes, abusive foster parents, constant loneliness ... On top of that I felt responsible for her death for years, so I know the guilt you're feeling." My words were barely above a whisper.

Glancing down, Kevin spoke to the square tombstone with his father's name chiseled across it. "I was just trying to make the world a better place. I didn't plan for it to happen like this. I loved him, you know. My dad. But he was so sad, riddled with guilt that ate him alive. He begged me to end his suffering. I did it *for* him."

"I get it. And I understand Jackson too—the child porn. But why my father? Why attack Tina? I thought you targeted child predators. Tina's just a child herself."

"Tina was about self-preservation. That was on you because I warned you. I was freaking out and needed to get you to back off." His hand dropped to his side. For a moment he was quiet, except for the sigh of a balmy evening breeze that ruffled my hair. "Your dad, well, you've got to know about his past by now, Ari. I hate to break it to you, but your father is about as innocent as mine was."

"Scott and my dad were just chess pieces, Kevin. Used by others. Neither of them actually committed the acts themselves."

"Go ahead and tell yourself that if it helps you sleep at night. But you're only lying to yourself and enabling them to keep abetting scumbags like George Battan. My father kidnapped a little girl, and whether he pulled the trigger or not, he still made a decision that directly put a girl into her grave. And then lied about it for two years. Your dad, well, his sins are a mile long. Abetting a known sex trafficker for decades, Ari. All your father had to do was tell the cops years ago what Battan was doing, and imagine all the lives that would have been spared. All the Marla Rivers who would be playing with dolls and running around the yard instead of rotting in unmarked graves.”

“Battan would have killed my dad if he snitched,” I protested.

“So? Do you realize how many soldiers go off to fight for their country knowing they might not return? They die willingly for the freedoms of others. Your father could have died nobly and with purpose. Instead he’ll die a coward because he was too selfish to put the lives of children ahead of his own.”

I had underestimated the depth of this old soul. “I get it. But why’s the only punishment death? Why can’t justice be served behind bars?”

“Prison’s too kind for monsters who victimize kids. I’m not saying it’s easy to willingly sacrifice yourself. I know I’m no hero—I fled the military when it got tough. And then I turned chickenshit when I was close to getting caught by you so I threatened innocent people. But to say our fathers didn’t deserve what they got is just fooling yourself.”

I felt his eyes probing me. For a long moment we said nothing, then I said the only thing that I hoped would get him to turn himself in.

“You preach justice. Sacrifice. You’ve taken two lives, three if my father doesn’t come out of his coma. What’s justice for you? Or doesn’t it apply to you?”

The knife slipped from his fingers, a *thud* on the grass at his feet. Kissing two fingers, he knelt down and rested his fingertips on his father’s named etched across the stone. Standing tall, he stepped toward me.

“Touché. I knew getting caught was inevitable. I’d hoped I’d stay ahead of you, but I can’t call myself a man if I can’t walk the talk.” Placing his rigid hand to the tip of his eyebrow, he saluted his father. “Love you, Dad. I’ll see you on the other side.”

Above us the clouds promenaded by. He followed me to

my car, holding himself with military bearing.

"You're not gonna kick my ass again and flee, are ya?" I said, breaking the tension.

He managed a wan smile. "No, ma'am."

That evening, Kevin, without preamble, answered every question, confessed to every crime, and steeled himself for the justice to come. I didn't sit in during the interrogation. I didn't read the written testimony. I had done my part, and now there was somewhere else more important I had to be.

Chapter 37
Ari

How come when I make pancakes they don't taste like this?" Tina asked across the booth from me.

We'd just finished an IHOP breakfast of all-you-can-eat pancakes, on me. My way of preemptively apologizing for not telling her about Giana sooner. I just hoped I'd buttered her up enough, figuratively speaking, to convince her to hear me out once I started explaining ... and begging for her to forgive me for my omissions.

"Because you don't use any of the ingredients that you're supposed to. Flavored coffee creamer isn't the same as milk, by the way. And there's a reason they sell measuring cups."

"Whatev. It's easier to just eat out than to cook anyway."

"And more expensive, too."

I wondered if Tina could taste the anxiety in the air like I could. I had been dreading this opening line for days. But it was now time, as Tina pushed a last bite of pancake around her plate, making circles in the syrup.

"Tina, I have some news for you."

She looked up at me, hope flickering in her eyes. "Giana?"

"Yeah, I found her."

Leaping up from the table, she hugged me awkwardly across the white Formica tabletop. Her arm knocked over a tiny vase holding a single red carnation. I hastily righted it as she withdrew.

"Thank you, Ari! I knew you could find her. My baby—I'm going to see my baby again!"

"There's more." I hated what I had to say next. "I don't think you should try to get her back."

"What? Why not? She's my baby, Ari. Mine. I gave birth to her!"

I could feel the eyes of fellow patrons turning in our direction as Tina's voice crescendoed.

"Tina, she's happy. She's with a good family. A *great* family that loves her. She's even got a little sister now. Somebody that looks up to her."

"Big effing deal. I would be a great mom to her."

"Really? What kind of family life could you give her? Home-cooked meals, helping her with homework, enrolling her in gymnastics, taking her to the park, arranging play dates? Do you really see yourself doing all that's needed to raise a child? Do you even know *how* to raise a child?"

"It's on-the-job training, Ari. I can learn as I go. That's what all first-time parents do."

"But you don't even have a job!"

"I'll get another one. I always do."

Tina could be so infuriating sometimes. What more could I expect from an eighteen-year-old?

"This is exactly my point. Tina, I love you, you know I do, but I'm trying to be a real friend to you here, a friend who's looking out for you and Giana. You want to just rip her away from what she already has—security, attention, stability? For what? You haven't even started your own life. You're always between jobs. You haven't finished high school. You're still finding out who you are."

"Oh, so I'm not good enough to be a mother?"

"I'm not saying that. You've been enslaved for the past decade, Tina! Have you forgotten that? Do you really want to drag a little girl through all that crap while you figure out who you are and what you want to do with your life? Especially when she's loved and treated so well by parents who give her everything she needs?"

Certainly Tina hadn't forgotten what it was like growing up imprisoned, thrown into a cycle of uncertainty, punishing starvation, and perpetual fear. And the abuse— what she endured I could never identify with. But she needed her own soul to heal before she could carry the burden of being responsible for another tiny budding life. I knew this because I was broken but mending too. It was my damaged life. It was her damaged life. It would be Giana's damaged life if Tina took her back. Removing Giana from her perfect family would be the death of life, the ruin of both their lives before they had even begun.

Tina raised her hand to block my face, to stop my words, to halt my appeal. I watched her oily pupils swallow the brown irises.

"I can't believe you're doing this to me, after all I've already lost." Her accusation was waspish, cruel.

"Please just consider an alternative. What if we talked to the parents about just letting you get to know Giana— but not seeking any kind of rights? You'd get to see her, be a part of her life, while she'd get to stay in a really good home environment. Kind of like an open adoption. Just think about it."

Tina turned away from me, the teenager in her showing itself as she silently pitched a bitch. There was no convincing her if her mind was set. This was the intersection where love and sacrifice met, but she would never see it that way. I knew this because we were cut from the same cloth, a cookie-cutter pattern of stubbornness. She was my reflection looking right back at me, after years of mulishly holding on to resentment toward my own parents. The silence between us couldn't be crossed. Space, that's what she needed. Hopefully to consider my offer, but more likely to fume against me.

I stood and grabbed my purse, placing a handful of one-dollar bills on the table for the tip.

"I love you, Tina. And I want what's best for you. I want you to live your life for yourself. But if raising Giana is what you want, fine, I'll help you do it. Because I love and support you, even when I think you're making a terrible mistake."

Even though it went against what I thought was right, I would do anything for Tina. For the one who saved me when I needed it. Now she was the one needing to be saved.

I headed down the aisle between the row of booths and tables, turning the corner to leave. As I exited the glass doors, through the window I caught a glimpse of the child that Tina still harbored—folded into the corner of our red leather booth, pouting and furious that she wasn't getting her way.

I had done everything I could to make my point, failing in the end. I really needed a smoke. Checking my emergency stash in my purse, I found one cigarette left and lit up. Two puffs in I felt guilty about it; I had promised Tristan no stress smoking and I'd been so good lately. Bad habits could be hard to kick, but I smothered the damn thing against the garbage can lid and tossed it inside, resenting that I had ever wanted to quit. Though maybe Tristan was right; I was stronger than I thought.

As I pressed the button to unlock my car, I heard my name.

"Ari!"

I turned around to see Tina chasing me down, her cheeks wet and her mascara running. By the time she caught up to me she was out of breath and heaving. "You're right. All I ever wanted was for Giana to be happy. If she's happy, then I've done my best for her. Sometimes we have to let those we love go if it's what's best for them …"

The softness of her words fluttered down around me, and I knew it was a message for me. A message about protecting our loved ones no matter the cost—the way I was protecting my father from his wrongs catching up with him.

It was time to stop protecting Burt and let the house of cards fall as they may.

MARLA RIVERS LAID TO REST, KILLER BROUGHT TO JUSTICE

Durham, North Carolina

After three long years, Bill and Justine Rivers finally received justice Monday as George Battan was sentenced for child sex trafficking and the murder of their ten-year-old daughter, Marla Rivers. In addition, Norman Bledsoe, long-time associate of Battan's, faces life in prison for multiple counts of murder and child abduction.

The ten-year-old girl went missing on December 6, 2013, disappearing from her bus stop. A witness testimony confirmed Marla spent two years enslaved in Battan's sex-trafficking ring. It wasn't until June 8, 2015, when a patron of a local park accidentally discovered her skeletal remains, later positively identified by authorities.

After an anonymous tip connected Battan to the murder, East Coast Bank manager Burt Wilburn was brought in for questioning. Shortly thereafter Wilburn was brutally attacked and lay comatose in Duke Hospital for several days. Upon regaining consciousness, he was held in protective custody based on evidence that linked him to Battan. While Battan was incarcerated for unrelated charges, Wilburn testified to working for Battan, corroborating details of Marla Rivers' abduction and abuse after being forced into a sex-trafficking ring led by Battan.

Battan faces twenty-five years in prison on multiple counts of sex trafficking of minors by force and conspiracy to commit murder. Burt Wilburn's trial is still pending. Bledsoe is awaiting trial and is currently being held without bond.

A memorial will be held for Marla Rivers. Marla's parents are currently establishing a nonprofit organization in their daughter's memory to aid victims of sex trafficking.

I folded the newspaper back up and tossed it on the coffee table where Tristan's socked feet were propped up. It was early morning, and we had stayed up all night talking and cuddling. Outside the dark galaxy had deflated into a slice of yellow, nudging the moon from its anchor in the sky while our voices chased away the stars and invited the sun to join us. A window hung open, inviting the fresh dawn air to enter.

"Looks like Battan will be behind bars for a long time. That's got to be a relief for you." Tristan unceremoniously pulled me against his lithe body stretched out across the sofa. I leaned into him, relishing the security and safety I felt when I was with him.

"Yeah, though I wish they'd fry him."

"At least he can't hurt any more kids." He paused, kissing my temple. "I'm sorry about your dad. I know that can't be easy for you watching him go to jail."

I shrugged. "It is what it is." What it was felt devastating, but I couldn't admit that. I was tired of feeling like a lost puppy. And if Kevin was right about anything, it was that my father deserved jail. He abetted criminals, profited from it, and contributed to the death of his own daughter. When I had last spoken to him, Dad seemed content with his lot, not a quiver of fear in his voice as he reminded me that his punishment was the only way to right his wrongs, but he did it all out of love for his family ... me included.

"At least things with my mom are getting better. Now with the threat of something happening to me gone, she actually wants to be my mother again. Crazy, right?"

Tristan nuzzled his nose against my neck. "Not crazy at all. Anyone who got to know you would love you like I do."

I scrambled around to look at him. Had I heard him right? He winked, his smile a riddle I couldn't figure out, his gaze hungry for a reply.

"Come again, Big Fudge?"

Cupping my chin in his hands, he searched my eyes

with his. "I love you, Ari. There, I said it. You don't have to say it back. But I wanted you to know how I felt."

"I ... I ..." I hadn't felt the capacity for love in such a long time. Any place where my heart and trust once resided long ago had been replaced with a vacant, gaping hole. But slowly Tina worked her way in, and now Tristan. Was this what love felt like—a sense of belonging, a guard-down freedom, an I'd-die-for-you loyalty? It was deeper than passion, more powerful than attraction.

"I love you too."

As he wrapped his arms around me, I knew I had found my soul mate. The one who encouraged me to pursue my dreams, who tolerated my stubborn streak and reckless impulses and compulsive quirks and weird friendships. I'd travel to the ends of the earth with this guy, and enjoy the cuts and bruises along the way, because for once someone was there to help mend me when I felt broken.

"By the way, I meant to tell you I love your new haircut," he added belatedly. Such a short ribbon of words, yet so meaningful. The observation meant almost as much to me as the *L* word, because it meant he was paying attention.

Tristan loved me and noticed me. Every little part of me.

Everything finally felt complete in my shattered but mending (and perpetually crazy) little world that I loved with every beat of my heart.

Epilogue
Ari

Our hands were clasped as we stood at Carli's grave, the first time we'd ever done this together since she died. Mother and daughter, relishing fond memories of the sweetest little girl we'd ever been lucky enough to know, even if only for a short while. We were mother and daughter again. While the years apart had created a schism between us, the resentment had started to erode. The bridge of healing was being built one baby step at a time.

The trees skirting the perimeter of the cemetery had begun to hibernate for the winter. My thoughts were pleated with various memories of Carli.

"Remember when Dad used to hide under Carli's bed in the morning and he'd grab her ankles when she got up?" I laughed at the memory of Carli screeching so loud that it'd set the neighbor's chihuahua to yapping.

"The poor little thing was traumatized to the point she was afraid to get out of bed some mornings and was late for breakfast." Mom chuckled as she said it, knowing that Carli adored her father's antics, cruel and unusual though they could be. "As punishment Carli made Daddy read you girls *Goodnight Moon* over and over again at bedtime for three months straight after that first time."

"He even used different voices every time he read it."

We stood in silent harmony, relishing the good memories. The only thing that would have made it perfect was if Carli and Dad could reminisce with us. In a way, Carli was, because I could feel her presence.

"How about when you first learned to ride your bike without training wheels? Do you remember that hill you were flying down, with Daddy running the whole way behind you?"

"Yeah, I was weaving all over the place. I'm pretty sure Dad had a mini heart attack after we got home." He had kissed my *owies* after I'd fallen and scraped my knees and elbows.

"*I* almost had a heart attack listening to you two tell me about it, and I wasn't even there. But you got back on that bike the next day, my tough girl."

"That's because Dad bribed me with ice cream."

"I'm going to miss him … while he's away."

I smiled. It was just like Mom to talk like Dad was going on a business trip, rather than to prison.

"You have me. I'll be here for you."

"I don't deserve you, sweetie."

They had given Dad a light sentence since he had agreed to testify against everyone involved and single-handedly shut down Battan's criminal organization. Norman Bledsoe lucked out with a life sentence for multiple homicides. If I had been on the jury, he would have been on death row. Despite everything my father had done in the past, I was proud of him for standing up like a man in the end, doing what was right in the face of a high price: his freedom. He could have hidden, ran, denied, lied … but he didn't. It was his parting gift before they dragged him away in handcuffs. And it was the best gift a daughter could ask for.

Except for this. This beautiful moment with my mother remembering life before.

The air exhaled a breeze that made me wrap my sweater tighter around me.

"You know, I'm proud of you, honey," Mom said. "And that boyfriend of yours—it's looking pretty serious. Do you think he's *the one*?"

She winked at me the way girlfriends do, the way Tina would when gossiping about a budding romance.

"Too early to tell yet. But he's definitely a keeper."

She squeezed me against her side. "After all the family lies and secrets and hurts and betrayals you've had to endure, you sure turned out pretty good, sweetie. And starting your own private investigation firm soon! So much to be excited about."

"Yeah, I'm afraid if I blink I'll wake up from this dream."

"Well, I have something for you." She rifled through her purse and pulled out an envelope, holding it out to me. "Here. It's a little down payment for when you open up your new business. I'm sure you'll need surveillance equipment and office space, so your father and I wanted you to have everything you needed to get started."

The envelope hung in the air between us, my fingers uncertain about accepting it. After all, Dad had been involved in some very shady dealings. How could I be sure I wasn't accepting the proceeds of his ill-gotten gains? *Screw it,* I thought. Hadn't we all suffered enough? I took the envelope. It contained a check. An incredibly generous one.

"Mom, you don't have to do this. With Dad in jail, don't you need to save your money?"

She shook her head. "I'm selling the house and downsizing. And this money isn't from your father's dealings. I've been saving up over the years—a private savings account. A gal's gotta have a rainy day fund, you know." She winked.

"Oh, you sly devil, you!" I laughed.

"I even got myself a nice little job in retail doing something I enjoy to keep me busy. I'll be fine. I insist you take this, Ari. Use it for your future ... with Tristan."

My eyes filled with happy tears. Throwing my arms around her neck, I gushed my thanks in a delirious mix of laughter and sniffles.

"Mom, this is so generous. I don't know what to say."

"Just say we'll never lose each other again. That's all I want."

Forgiveness was an easy gift to give her as we hugged in the warm sunshine, her burnt orange sweater soft against my cheek. But the scars still marked me, created me, toughened me. I could forgive, maybe even forget a little more each day, but it would take time.

I was starting a new life, filling it with a reunited family, a delicious romance, and the challenges and excitement of a dream career, and I couldn't wait to see what my future would bring me. I was ready for just about anything.

Across town Eve Baxter nursed her infant while Giana pieced together an animal puzzle on the floor. In Eve's hand was a letter they'd received, addressed in perfect cursive to *Giana on your 18th birthday.*

Eve hesitated to open it, fearing what could possibly be inside. The significance of the birthday weighed heavily on her. They had always planned on telling Giana that she was adopted, but as the months fell away one by one, the decision of when and how to bring it up slipped further out of thought. Why complicate things for a child so young? Would she even understand what it all meant? What if she didn't want Eve as her mother anymore? And so the fears drove her to silence.

But truth always had a way of resurfacing. And Eve's nauseous gut told her this letter was exactly that.

Sliding her finger across the sealed edge, she opened it up and pulled out a single page framed in rainbows, unicorns, and hearts. Perhaps it wasn't hers to read, but she needed to know what some stranger was sending her daughter.

And so she read, the words artfully scrawled down the page:

Dear Giana:

Now that you're eighteen years old, it's time you met me. I've spent your entire life thinking about you, wondering what kind of woman you've grown up to be, hoping you're happy, loving you with every bone in my body.

My name is Tina Alvarez, and I'm your biological mother.

When I first held you in my arms, I knew at that very moment you had completed my life. You made me whole. You healed my broken heart. I'd been in a horrible situation (I'll tell you more about it if you decide you want to meet me), but having you was the one beautiful miracle I got to experience in my life.

You might be wondering why I gave you up. The sad truth is that you were stolen from me—not by your parents, in case you were wondering. But by someone who will never be able to steal another child again. With the help of a friend I found you again when you were three years old, but I saw how happy you were with your new family, the Baxters. I could tell how much they love you. How could I compete with them—a happily married couple, a sibling for you to play with, a nice home? So I had a decision to make.

I could involve myself in your life and complicate things for you, or I could let you grow up with the perfect life you deserved. It wasn't easy walking away; I regretted it daily. But I knew it was best for you, especially after all I'd gone through and how much I needed to mend myself on my own before I could ever be worth your love.

Now that you're an adult, I hope you'd be willing to meet me. I'd like to get to know you. I want to be there for you, maybe not as a mother since you already have a good one, but as a friend. As someone who truly loves you. No matter how much time passes, you will always be the baby girl I held in my arms, the one who breathed life back into me. By the time you read this I don't know where I'll live or if I'll have a family, but know that I'll always be waiting for you, watching over you, making sure you're taken care of. Consider me your guardian angel.

I love you, Giana. And I hope you'll give me a chance to show it when you're ready.

Much love,
Tina Alvarez

Eve folded the letter and slid it back into the envelope. Unlatching the baby, Eve shifted her against her shoulder. "I'll be right back, sweetie," she said, rising from her chair and patting Giana on the head. "Save the last piece of the puzzle for me, okay?"

"Of course, Mommy. You always get to do the last piece," Giana affirmed, looking up at her with a smile.

Eve headed upstairs to Giana's room, then opened her closet door. Reaching up awkwardly, her fingertips fumbled against a pink-painted wooden box, until her tiptoes gave her just enough height to grab the corner. Pulling the box down, she placed it on the bed and lifted the metal latch. Inside was a collection of newborn baby photos, the outfit they had first received Giana in, and other sentimental things she had collected over the years. Placing the letter inside, she closed the box and returned it to its shelf.

"I promise you'll be reunited," she whispered to the empty room. She knew what it was like to love a child so much that it hurt and hated that a mother was forced to suffer the loss of her daughter.

Moving across the hallway, she laid the baby on the bed and opened her bedside drawer. Inside she found an empty journal that Giana had made her for Mother's Day, decorated with pressed flower petals on the cover, shiny and still clinging to their colors under the lamination. Opening it up, she grabbed a pen and began to write:

Dear Tina:

Thank you for the gift of letting me raise Giana. So that you don't have to miss out on her childhood, I want to chronicle her life for you. I'd love for you to get to know her so that when the time is right for you to meet in person, you'll have shared in the memories she's created with us.

Giana turns four soon. She's a beautiful little girl, so smart too. She's already reading short words, her favorites being dog, cat, *and pretty much any animal. And puzzles— she loves puzzles. We have a tradition where she saves the last piece of the puzzle for Mommy or Daddy. One day I hope you'll get to fill in that last piece of the puzzle in her life.*

Ever grateful,
Eve

Author's Note

It was a trauma I would never get over, even now, years later. I had just popped out my fourth baby, and my hands were full. I was sleep-deprived, lonely, and with my oldest child only five, I felt like I was running a marathon just to keep up with daily life.

My oldest was helping Daddy on a home project while I entertained the little ones. My three-year-old autistic son wanted to go outside, so I told him to wait while Mommy changed the newborn's dirty diaper. Except that my son wasn't the best at following directions.

It only took me about two minutes to change the diaper—I'd had lots of practice over the years. But two minutes was all it took for my son to unlatch the deadbolt and slip out the front door, guiding his one-year-old sister by the hand down the front porch into the yard.

Now, we had a five-acre farm and our driveway was pretty long, so when I realized they had snuck out, I figured they'd be playing in the henhouse or in the barn, where they always explored. Except by the time I searched both places, they were nowhere to be found.

This is when the panic set in.

This was when a nightmare becomes reality for a mother.

I was fortunate that they hadn't wandered too far up our street, thankfully into the hands of a kind stranger who kept them safe until I sprinted up there, baby bouncing on my chest, while I screamed their names. The problem with an autistic child is they don't always respond back when you call, and the return of silence is petrifying.

That day marked the first time I understood how easily a child could get abducted. What if that man hadn't been so kind? What if he had taken them? The two minutes I lost track of them could have been two minutes of him speeding off with my children in tow.

Abductions happen. I often read about them in the news, but I hadn't lived that possibility of it happening to me until that moment.

In *The Death of Life,* I wanted justice for all the children who don't make it home into their mother's safe arms. It's a small consolation for their loss, but for those horrible minutes when I felt that hysteria, worried about a tragic ending, I understood them.

Few children who are kidnapped have a happy ending like Tina's daughter, Giana. For all the Kats and Marlas in the world, your voices are heard, you are not forgotten. I hope as a society we can bring justice to those who hurt children and raise our own kids to be people who will spread the reach of love in a world of hurt.

I hope you enjoyed *The Death of Life* and will walk away from it knowing that there are people like Ari Wilburn who are passionate about changing the world for the better, no matter what the world has done to them. Let's do all we can to help them achieve this goal. Hugs to you all!

Acknowledgements

When someone offers to help me, I don't decline it. As a writer-editor-mother-wife-farmer-zookeeper-multi-tasker, I'll take whatever support I can get. I'm fortunate enough to have an amazing support team.

My husband is always at the top of my praise list. I wouldn't have become a writer without his encouragement, and I wouldn't have the time to write if he didn't watch the kids for me weekend after weekend, evening after evening. He's my everything. Thank you, honey, for pushing me to keep going.

Second on the list is always you, my amazing fans. If you didn't buy my books, I couldn't afford to invest so much time into this dream. You're who I do this all for!

Of course I could never forget to include my family and friends—you have served so faithfully as my beta readers, my editors, and my support group. It's been an incredible journey that I wouldn't have wanted to venture on without you.

Thank you to my editor Kevin Cook at Proofed to Perfection, the best among the best, for helping me bring my thoughts to life and prepping my stories for the public.

To the littlest fans I have, my amazing children: Talia, Kainen, Kiara, and Ariana. You make me laugh, cry, tear my hair out, feel like a kid again, and give me greater life purpose. Thank you for being the greatest gifts of all.

A Final Word...

If you'd like to be notified of my upcoming releases or enter my giveaways, join my mailing list at www.pamelacrane.com for chances to win free prizes and pre-release offers.

PAMELA CRANE: Horse tamer. Book editor. Mom of four. Reading addict. Literary reviewer. These are just a few of the roles I play, and I relish them all. I'm a proud mama of a crazy brood that keeps me on my toes, and I can't turn away stray animals, which is how I ended up with a farm full of misfit pets. I hope they never find a cure for my reading addiction, because it's what keeps me sane. I love writing women's fiction and anything mystery or psychological thriller, because the crazier the characters, the more sane I feel!

Discover more books at

www.pamelacrane.com